# BE THE ONE

## FIREWEED HARBOR SERIES

# J.H. CROIX

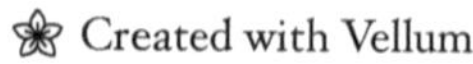 Created with Vellum

*To our sweet B.*

**Sign up for my newsletter for information on new releases & get a FREE copy of one of my books!**

*http://jhcroixauthor.com/subscribe/*

**Follow me!**

*jhcroix@jhcroix.com*

*https://amazon.com/author/jhcroix*

*https://www.bookbub.com/authors/j-h-croix*

*https://www.facebook.com/jhcroix*

*https://www.instagram.com/jhcroix/*

# Chapter One

# QUINN

"I invested everything, and now we're on track to be the most profitable start-up in..."

"*Blah, blah, blah, blah...*" That was basically all I heard.

This guy had dominated the conversation so thoroughly that he'd become that voice from the cartoons that faded into unintelligible repetitive sounds.

This guy had matched with me on a dating app. I didn't even remember which one at this point. I thought this night would never end. Reaching a point of a bored kind of panic and restlessness, I kept crossing and uncrossing my legs under the table.

"Quinn?" the man prompted.

I had to mentally scramble for his name. Oh right, this was Brad.

"Yes?" I replied, my tone perfectly polite as I pasted a tight smile on my face.

Brad cocked his head to the side. He was handsome enough, objectively speaking, with straight, short blond hair and brown eyes with sharp features. I felt nothing, not even a glimmer of a spark. Dating apps were shit. I should've known I didn't need to waste my time on this guy or any guy.

Yet I was trying and trying and trying to find someone. Dating in the tiny fishbowl of Fireweed Harbor, Alaska, my hometown, was limited. Pickings were slim enough to blow away with a puff of air.

"Did you even hear what I said?" he returned sharply.

"I'm sorry, I'm a little distracted." It wasn't like I needed this date to go anywhere. I figured I might as well be honest.

Brad nodded. "Fair enough. Shall we split the check?"

Just then, I felt a prickle of awareness chase up my spine. And I knew, I *knew*, without knowing, that Kenan Cannon was somewhere nearby. Which was insane. Because I was in Seattle, and he should've been back in Fireweed Harbor.

Seconds later, he stopped beside the table, his alert eyes landing on mine. "Hello there, Quinn."

Kenan was one of my closest friends. I'd never, repeat that *never*, been attracted to him until a few months ago when this weird thing happened one night. I was still convinced it had been a fluke, except that stupid flare of chemistry was now simmering between us like molten lava.

My belly fluttered, and my pulse kicked up its heels before taking off at a fast gallop.

"Oh, hi!" I squeaked, silently cursing as soon as my voice came out. I didn't squeak.

I gestured to Brad. "This is Brad. Brad, Kenan Cannon." My hand swung toward Kenan. I scrambled inside, trying to think of some reason Kenan was here.

Brad's brows hitched up, a calculating glint entering his eyes. He stood quickly, holding out his hand. "Hi, nice to meet you. Brad Smith. I'm heading up…"

My brain turned up the static. I was so very weary of listening to Brad talk about his business.

"I heard Fireweed Industries moved their headquarters out of Seattle," Brad was saying as I forced my brain to focus again. He released Kenan's hand.

Kenan nodded. "We did. Like Quinn, I'm traveling. We still keep a small office here. I'm kind of the do-everything guy for our corporation." His gaze caught mine. "Quinn's here handling a legal matter for us, and I'm coordinating with a few of our distribution warehouses."

Brad nodded along. "Well, I'd love to set up a meeting. I know you all invest in various ventures, and I'd love the opportunity to explain ours to you."

It was all I could do not to groan aloud. Just when I thought this date would end, Kenan had to show up and make the guy want to linger.

I felt Kenan's gaze on me. I almost snorted when I saw the knowing look in his eyes. He totally knew I was ready to get the hell out of here.

He glanced at Brad. "I don't have time tonight, but you can send me an email. It's on our website. I'll follow up if it looks like something we might be interested in. Meanwhile, I don't want to interrupt."

Oh. My. God. Instead of saving me from this endless, boring date, he was going to excuse himself? What the fuck?

I stood so fast that my thighs bumped into the table, jostling my now empty glass of wine. "We were just about to get the check," I said swiftly.

Kenan's eyes met mine again, and I battled to keep my cheeks from burning up. Between my hormones doing gymnastics and my annoyance with Brad, composure was nowhere to be found. Conveniently, the server was walking by and heard what I said. He stopped beside us. "I've got the check right here. Are you—"

I cut in. "Two checks, please."

His expression didn't even twitch. He had heard Brad running on every time he stopped by the table, so I sensed he took pity on me when his eyes met mine. Lifting a handheld tablet, he quickly tapped on the screen, then printed out a receipt and handed it to me. I paid right there on the spot while Brad continued to try to chat up Kenan.

I mentally excused myself from being rude. "Nice to see you tonight, Kenan. Good to meet you, Brad. You take care now." I nodded at them both.

I wouldn't have been surprised if dust kicked up behind my heels as I walked away from the table. I didn't hear Kenan say goodbye to Brad, but I knew he was behind me a moment later because I could feel him. The damn man.

Normally, I would've been relieved to see him. I wanted to vent to him about my nightmare of a date and lament my poor dating prospects in Fireweed Harbor. But lately, every time we spent time together, it ended with me flustered and spun tight inside with arousal. It was disconcerting and maddening, to say the least.

*Chapter Two*

# KENAN

*Minutes earlier*

Quinn Blackthorn stared at me beside the table, her eyes practically shooting sparks. I couldn't believe my luck. I would never, *fucking ever*, admit to her that I had seen her seated at this table through a window outside and couldn't resist coming in. Even from a distance, I'd known she was annoyed with this Brad guy. I knew Quinn well, maybe too well. The set of her jaw and the boredom written all over her face had given her away.

I would also never, *fucking ever*, admit to her that I had a thing for her. I didn't know what the hell to do about it, and I kept telling myself it would pass. Crazy drumbeats of lust kicked up every time we were near each other. It had only been a month since it happened, and I was convinced it was a fluke.

Fortunately, I was a busy guy, and Quinn was a workaholic. Even though we usually got together at least once a week or so, I'd been successfully avoiding her and hoped she hadn't noticed. Somehow, seeing her here in Seattle—on a date, for crying out loud—had been irresistible.

A moment later, Quinn had spun away and was disappearing with swift strides through the restaurant. I was pretty sure she was trying to shake me. She was out of luck on that count. I had a room beside her at the hotel. I walked briskly to catch up with her.

I met her and slowed my stride to match her pace. Quinn came to a stop and blinked when she looked up at me. Yet again, I noticed how thick her eyelashes were. Until recently, I could honestly say I'd never noticed my friend's eyelashes.

I shifted on my feet, hoping against hope that Quinn had not noticed my arousal. Lately, it was a war of wills between my brain and body whenever I was around her. Which was seriously fucking inconvenient because she was my best friend.

It had all started at Blake's wedding. Something misfired in the universe that day. I'd seen Quinn at the reception afterward, a perfectly normal and expected encounter. In a matter of mere seconds, it felt as if lightning had shot down from the sky and set my body alight with a sizzling need for her.

She was practically family. I didn't remember not knowing her. Although we'd always been friendly, after we'd both moved away for college and so on and returned to our small hometown, we'd become close friends.

She was the friend I turned to when I needed to talk. I could talk with her in a way I couldn't with anyone else, even my family. It wasn't that I didn't love my family. It was more that sometimes you just needed someone who wasn't in the thick of it. Lord knows, being one of seven siblings with a few tangled family messes in our past, something was always going on.

When she stopped at the intersection to look up at me, that feeling slammed into me—it felt like a fist thudded into my chest and sent sensation outward in a blast. Electricity flickered between us, tightening every cell in my body as they fired with anticipation and restless need.

Quinn was stunning, and she was annoyed. Her gorgeous hazel eyes narrowed. I loved the way her nose turned up at the end and her bow-shaped lips. They were just, well, kissable was the only word that came to mind. And holy hell did I want to kiss her.

I was relieved when the light changed, and we resumed walking. Because I was *that* fucking close to kissing her.

Her fitted skirt flared just above her knees, and she'd paired it with tall boots. No heels for Quinn. She was too practical for that. Her jacket hung open, and I noticed, yet again when we stopped at another intersection, that she was wearing a silky blouse. I could see the lace of her bra peeking out at the edge when she lifted a hand to brush her hair back impatiently.

Fuck me. I wanted to unbutton her blouse. With my teeth. To peel it back and see what lay hidden behind it.

It wasn't that I didn't know Quinn had curves. I'd just never paid attention to them. Now, I was dying to know how the weight of one of her plump breasts would feel cupped in my palm. I wanted to know how pink her nipples were and how she might sound if I teased her and sucked one into my mouth.

"Kenan?" Quinn waved a hand in front of my face.

I'd completely spaced out and had no idea what she'd just said, if anything. I decided to play it off.

"Light changed," I said quickly. "Race you to the hotel."

Moments later, we were both out of breath when we stopped in front of the hotel. She leaned over to tug her skirt down a little, giving me a revealing glimpse of the shadowed valley between her breasts. I could see the curves, and my cock swelled.

Fuck. I needed to get a grip and fast.

# Chapter Three

# QUINN

"Where did you meet Brad?" he drawled, his tone teasing and sly.

We'd called it a tie with our impromptu race to the hotel entrance. We'd just caught our breath and waited inside the crowded area outside the elevators.

"Dating app," I ground out. "We matched, and I thought I might see how it went."

"And how did it go?"

I turned to look up at him and rolled my eyes. "Awful. He's really into himself."

Kenan chuckled, and the sound sent a hot shiver chasing over my skin. "I'll look forward to his email. I could put in a good word for you. He seems handsome enough," he offered with a shrug, his tone drier than chalk.

"Oh my God. Do not put in a good word for me," I muttered. "I do *not* want to go on another date with him. *Ever*. I don't like dating apps, but I do like how you can only communicate in them at first. He doesn't even have my number. Now, because you showed up at our table, I'm worried he's going to try to stay in touch because he thinks I'll be a good connection with Fire-weed Industries."

"Didn't he know you worked for us?" Kenan prompted

"I didn't tell him. I just told him I did corporate law. That was enough information."

"Hmm," he replied vaguely.

I was resigned to my fate. Kenan was going to want to get a drink together, and then I'd be stuck with him and wrestling with my annoying attraction to him.

A few minutes later, we stepped into the elevator together. "Which floor?" he asked.

Glancing up, I tried to call on my old indifference. Well, not indifference specifically. He *was* one of my closest friends. I didn't feel indifferent, but there had been no spark before, like zero, zilch. I had never, *ever*, expected to feel anything when I looked at my friend. His sharp, perceptive blue gaze held mine.

Kenan was one of seven siblings in the vaunted Cannon family from my small hometown. The Cannons were, by far, the wealthiest family in town. They were all nice. Kenan was smack in the middle with his twin brother, Adam. They weren't identical twins. Unlike most of his siblings who had dark blond hair and gray eyes, Kenan had inherited his mother's almost black hair and startlingly bright blue eyes.

Because life was fucking unfair, he was also hand-some. He had sharp cheekbones and a straight nose, paired with full sensual lips that always looked as if he was on the verge of a smile.

As if to agree with my point, one corner of his lips kicked up, sending my belly into a dizzying flip. "Quinn? What floor?"

"Seven," I said, my voice coming out a little raspy.

For God's sake, the man was making me breathless.

I didn't get breathless. I had all but given up on thinking I'd ever have anything like romance in my life. Oh, I dated, or I tried. I'd struggled since high school to shake the cloak of being the class nerd, too bookish for anyone to notice.

Kenan had been popular in high school. Not an asshole, but very popular and definitely a catch. Somehow, we'd ended up friends. To this day, I wasn't really sure how. I had enough sense to know my friendship with him likely protected me from too much teasing back then. We had a few classes together, and our parents were friends because my father had been one of the main lawyers for Fireweed Industries back in the day. I'd slipped right into the same role after my father had decided to cut back on his schedule.

"We're on the same floor," he said with an easy grin.

"I didn't know you were going to be down here," I replied.

Kenan tapped the button on the elevator. "I didn't either. Rhys was supposed to come, but something came up, so I offered to come in his place. We have two new distributors down here, so paperwork and meetings. All that stuff that you love."

His grin was sly when he glanced over. He'd been teasing me more than usual lately about working too much. It typically wouldn't get to me, but I was feeling sensitive about it. I loved my job. I legitimately enjoyed it, but I wanted to start a family. More than marriage, I wanted children. I finally started doing the dating app dance because I figured I had two options. Find a man and have children that way, or try in vitro fertilization via a sperm donor. After tonight's date with Brad, I was pretty sure I was ready for door number two.

I'd already looked into the process. Surreptitiously, mind you. I had my regular doctor in Fireweed Harbor, and she referred me to the fertility clinic in Juneau. I knew what I needed to do, I just needed to resign myself to starting the process. Maybe it was best. Brad was my latest disappointing date.

I forced myself to focus. "Oh," I said. "I'm assuming Rhys forwarded you all the information I sent him for that?"

"Of course he did," Kenan returned with an exaggerated brow waggle. "You know my brother, he's always on top of things. He's kind of like you."

"You're on top of things too," I pointed out.

Even though Kenan never spoke of it, I knew he was sensitive about feeling like he wasn't taken as seriously as his brothers. With his oldest brother Rhys the CEO of their family's corporation, and the next one in line, Blake, managing the production and distribution arm of the company, and then his own twin being the numbers guy as the CFO, Kenan had a less defined role in the company. I personally knew his job title was executive. As one of the main lawyers for the corporation, all of that stuff flowed through me from human resources.

Kenan did whatever needed to be done. He was sharp, too smart for his own good, but he didn't realize it. He covered up his uncertainty around that by always keeping things light and funny. I didn't realize I'd sighed out loud until he prompted, "What was that for? You sound downright weary, Quinn."

I glanced up at him, ignoring the flutter of butterflies in my belly. "Nothing." Just then, my stomach growled audibly, and I slapped my palm over it. "Dinner wasn't great. I just wanted to get out of there, so all I had was a few bites of the appetizer, and that was two hours ago."

"Brad talked about himself for two hours?" Kenan turned, resting his hips against the railing in the elevator as it came to a stop for a family to file out.

I rolled my eyes. "That he did. He likes himself," I said sarcastically.

There. I could get us back on safe ground. Just joke about my bad date and lament dating in Fireweed Harbor.

"Well, I haven't eaten dinner. Let's get room service," Kenan suggested.

"You don't want to go down to the restaurant?" I asked just as the elevator stopped on a different floor and a couple stepped in.

The elevator began moving as Kenan replied, "Not really. There's supposed to be a football game on. I'd rather kick back and relax. What do you say?"

I should've said no, but we were friends, so I usually would say yes. I didn't want him to get suspicious. At all.

"Sure." I shrugged lightly. The elevator stopped at another floor before we finally got off on ours.

"Where is your room?" I asked.

We had fallen into step, heading in the same direction. "702."

"Oh. You're beside me."

"Tish must've made the reservations for you and Rhys at the same time. She switched his room to mine." Tish Reeves was the lead executive assistant at Fireweed Industries and helped coordinate travel for staff.

"Mmm," was all I could manage in reply.

We stopped at the doors to our rooms. "Maybe we

have a connecting door," he said. "Your room or mine?"

I tried to ignore the way my pulse kept revving and the way heat spun fire through my veins.

"You pick," I rasped.

"I'll come to yours. I already left my suitcase on my bed. It'll look messy. I know your room will be tidy."

I bit my lip to keep from laughing. "Do you need to go into your room first?" I asked as I waved my key card in front of the lock.

"Nope." He leaned a shoulder against the wall.

When my attempt to get the lock to open didn't work, I waved the key card again, muttering, "I hate these things. It's bad enough when we used to slide them in, but now you have to wave it just so."

After two more tries, Kenan held out his palm. "Hand it over, Quinn. That was three tries. Let me have a go at it."

Our fingers brushed as I handed him the key card. It felt like sparks leaped where we touched. The sensation sizzled up my arm, spinning into my body.

A moment later, he deftly moved it across the sensor pad, the light turned green, and the lock clicked open. "See, easy," he teased.

"Kenan, the great key card door opener," I returned dryly, relieved that I could at least slip into our easy banter.

Maybe an hour or so later, we had eaten, and Kenan had lavishly tipped our server when he came to collect the cart of empty plates. I'd been too nervous to eat much, but he'd scarfed down a whole plate of pasta with a cream sauce.

Kenan flopped back down on the couch beside me, while I tried to think of how to get him out of my room. I was flustered, my skin almost itchy from the prickly heat of desire that just wouldn't dissipate.

We had both kicked our shoes off. Kenan wore jeans with an untucked button-down shirt. My eyes lingered on the vee of skin exposed just above where his collar fell open. He was the kind of guy who always seemed a little bronzed, as if the sun shone just for him all year long, even in the long winters of Alaska. He wasn't a vain man. I knew he didn't go out of his way to stay tan.

He stretched his arm across the back of the loveseat. My room had a seating area, but it wasn't big. Just a small loveseat and another single chair. A part of me wanted to leap out of the loveseat and stay in the chair so an entire coffee table remained between us. But that might draw attention.

Kenan was definitely an eyebrow raiser. He'd given me a look. Hell, he communicated with his eyebrows arching, one or the other up, waggling them and the like.

"So that's a no to Brad?" he prompted.

I didn't even bother to deny it as I nodded. "Definitely. I think I'm going to give up on trying to date. Fireweed Harbor is too small, and I hate dating apps."

"Now, now, don't give up. I'm sure I can find a guy for you."

When I looked his way, he actually appeared serious.

"No, no, no, no, no!" I said swiftly, shaking my head to punctuate each word. "You focus on yourself. Plus—" I waved a hand airily. "It's your turn."

"My turn for what?"

"To fall in love and get married. Rhys and Haven already have a baby. And Blake is in love with Fiona. It's your turn."

# Chapter Four

# KENAN

I stared down at my friend. "It's definitely not my turn. You know I'm not all about that."

Quinn cocked her head to the side, studying me. I hated how well she knew me and how it felt like she could see straight into my heart. She shrugged. "You never know."

"Just like you never know," I lobbed back at her. "Maybe you'll find the right guy in Fireweed Harbor." My hand rested beside her shoulder, and my fingers literally itched to touch her.

She rolled her eyes. "I seriously doubt that."

Before I could respond, she stood from the couch so quickly that her knee bumped into the coffee table. She let out a little yelp, stumbling back toward the small loveseat.

I wasn't thinking when I reached out reflexively to steady her. One hand landed on her hip and the other on the side of her waist. "Easy there," I murmured.

She looked down at me, biting her bottom lip.

"Your knee okay?" I prompted, trying to ignore my

aching need and the fact that my hands were on her, and I couldn't seem to pull them away.

She blinked with her nod. Her lashes fell, and she glanced down. I suddenly made a decision. Maybe I just needed to kiss her, then I would realize this was nothing. It would snap us out of this place. While neither of us had said a single word about it, I sensed she felt the same fiery snap and crackle between us whenever we were together.

"C'mere," I murmured as I shifted forward.

Her gaze whipped to mine, her eyes widening. "Huh?"

I slid one hand around her waist, coaxing her closer. She didn't resist. A second later, she stood between my knees. With me seated, we were almost eye to eye. My heart pounded so hard that I could hear the beat of it rushing in my ears.

"Why?" she whispered.

"I just want to test a theory."

"A theory?"

Fuck me. Her low, throaty voice was going to slay me.

"I'm going to kiss you. Then I'll remember this weird thing between us is all in my head."

For a split second, I could've sworn I saw hurt flash in her eyes. She lifted her chin, her jaw tightening. "It's definitely all in your head. Let's test that theory. That way you can stop avoiding me."

Oh, she just *had* to go and fling that shot across the bow.

I coaxed her even closer until I could feel the heat of her body. We stared at each other, and my body felt on fire, nearly vibrating with the force of electricity shimmering between us.

My hand was still resting on her hip, and I could

feel the soft give of the curve there. I tried to take a steadying breath, but I couldn't get much air in, and my lungs felt tight.

Quinn just stared at me. I sensed she was daring me to make the first move. In the end, I didn't know who moved first, all I knew was our lips met. Once again, it felt like lightning shot down from the sky between us, setting us on fire. I told myself it was just going to be a brief kiss. That was it.

But then, she made this little sound in the back of her throat, and her lips were so soft, so plump and inviting. I lingered, waiting for reality to snap into place and for me to remember she was just my friend and nothing more.

Yet that was not what happened, not even close. In another moment, I had fit my mouth over hers, and my hand slid around her waist as the other tangled in her hair. I kissed her as if my very life depended on it. She tasted sweet and a little tart, just how I would imagine because it was her personality. She had a huge heart but a sharp edge to her. She was so fucking smart.

Her tongue tangled with mine, and I deepened our kiss, pulling her closer. Next thing I knew, she straddled me, and I could feel the heat of her core as she restlessly rocked over the hard ridge of my arousal. It was almost unbearable. Holy fucking hell. I wanted to be inside her so bad I didn't know if I could stop it before we got to that point.

Somehow, some-fucking-how, we broke apart and simply stared at each other. My heart still pounded, and I was so tight with need, I almost couldn't breathe. Her eyes were wide, dark pools of desire. She looked as stunned as I felt.

# Chapter Five

# QUINN

*Later that night*

Somehow, I honestly didn't know how, I got myself off Kenan's lap, mortified to discover that my arousal had left my panties drenched. Even worse, I'd been practically writhing with abandon on his lap. *Kenan's lap!* The only saving grace—and I wasn't sure if this made it better or worse—was that I knew he was aroused as well. I'd been rocking over his hard cock, and I could feel it pulse under me even through the rough fabric of his jeans.

My mind frantically replayed the moments following me scrambling off Kenan's lap. We'd stared at each other, our chests heaving, both of us clearly flustered. My thoughts bounced to the way it felt to kiss him.

I experienced another blaze of heat from head to toe, and I was just lying in bed alone. I scrambled to gather my tattered composure. I knew Kenan well enough to know he was also out of sorts and probably shocked beyond measure. The knowledge that he was in the room beside me burned like a lump of hot coal inside. This wasn't the first time we'd been in the same location traveling for Fireweed Industries.

We often traveled together. Typically, we had dinner together. I might be watching a show and send him amusing texts about it. Frantic for some kind of distraction, I shimmied back, propping the pillows behind me on the headboard and reaching for the remote on the bedside table.

I began scrolling through the channels to find something to watch, before finally settling on a light comedy.

"There," I said out loud. "It was just a kiss. Totally a fluke."

I groaned as my head fell back against the head-board. That had probably been the best kiss of my life. Kenan had no clue. I couldn't even imagine what he might think if he ever discovered my plans. We told each other almost everything. Almost.

I'd been a true geek in high school—smart, intro-verted, bookish, and awkward looking. It wasn't that I cared all that much about what anyone else thought. I hadn't had a high school boyfriend, and by the time I grew out of my awkwardness, I was busy in college. I dated a little bit, but the hookup scene didn't suit me, at all. Not because I was a prude or judged anyone, but rather, it just wasn't for me.

Dating was a special version of hell. I loved living in a small town for the most part. I'd jumped at the chance to move back home and work in my parents' law practice. I'd been thrilled when my dad told me he wanted to step back from being the leading lawyer for Fireweed Industries. I had an office right there in the corporation. Kenan and I had been casual friends in high school, born of our parents being friends and spending plenty of time together.

With his role in the corporation, he traveled a lot and tended to be the one they called upon to solve problems. Whenever there was a legal issue, we were often thrown together. Over the past five years or so, we had become close friends.

Now, I'd gone and kissed him, and I was *still* hot and bothered by it.

I forced my attention back to the sitcom, managing to distract myself for a few minutes. Until a couple on the show, who were totally in the friend zone, started kissing. "What the fuck?" I whispered to myself.

I kicked the sheets off and strode into the shower. A blast of cold water snapped through the heat simmering inside my body since that ill-fated kiss.

I told myself I'd get over it. I'd see Kenan in the morning and realize how crazy it had been.

# Chapter Six

# KENAN

*Three days later*

"There you are," Rhys commented as I walked into his office.

"Here I am." I held my arms out as I crossed the room, asking, "Mind if I have a cup of coffee?"

"Of course not. Better yet, why don't we walk down to Spill the Beans together?"

I stopped beside the table in my brother's office where a half-full coffee pot sat.

"Their coffee is better than that," he pointed out. He stood from his desk as he nudged his chin in the direction of the coffee pot.

"Sounds good." I wasn't going to pass up a chance for fucking amazing coffee.

Rhys snagged his jacket off a chair and shrugged into it. Although my brother was the CEO of our family's corporation, an international conglomerate, he typically wore jeans and a long-sleeved Henley to the office.

As he fell into step beside me when we began walking down the hallway, I glanced over. "That's a nice change from Seattle, isn't it?"

"What do you mean?" he asked as he crested the top of the stairs.

Our footsteps echoed down the stairwell. "In Seattle, the downtown district is mostly people wearing suits. I mean, sure, you could've gotten away with jeans, but not when you went to meetings and such."

Rhys grinned as we reached the bottom stair. "It's good to be home."

We pushed through the double doors together just as a cold gust of wind blew by. Rhys zipped his jacket up, adding, "Winter's here. Almost."

We walked down the sidewalk together. I replied, "Technically, winter isn't here until the winter solstice in December. But this is Alaska. We should have some snow before Thanksgiving."

The tension bundled in my neck and shoulders eased with every step away from our corporation's main offices here in Fireweed Harbor. We had our headquarters in Seattle for a while, and Rhys lived down there full-time. I ended up being there about half the year then.

We'd decided to keep nothing more than a bare-bones office for us there. With online capacity, we didn't need our headquarters there. I had busied myself in that office while I avoided coming home for a few days because of that kiss with Quinn. Every time I thought about it, need burned through me like a brushfire.

We'd seen each other the following morning and tried to play it cool. Except every time I looked at her mouth, I remembered what it felt like. I remembered the way her tongue boldly teased against mine. The way her body felt soft and lush in my lap.

I'd driven her to the airport, lying when I told her my trip was a few days longer than hers. I'd even had to call Rhys's assistant, Tish, to make a quick change to my flight. I told Quinn something had come up. I knew she didn't believe me.

Before that kiss, she would've been skeptical. She probably would've asked me if I was staying longer because I had a date. I knew things had changed when all she did was nod and let me lie about something so minor.

I seriously valued my friendship with Quinn and didn't want to fuck it up, yet I feared we already had. My whole purpose with that kiss had been to show myself that my abrupt lust for her had been all in my mind. That hadn't worked. Not even close.

I looked around as we walked down the sidewalk in Fireweed Harbor. The downtown area was cute with shops and storefronts with brightly colored signs. A few businesses were ahead of the curve and already decorating for the upcoming holidays.

Fireweed Harbor was in Southeast Alaska along the pristine shores of the famed Inside Passage. The town was nestled at the base of the mountains with snow-covered peaks surrounding it, a glacier visible nearby, a few islands out in the ocean, and a picturesque harbor with boats, eagles, and seagulls calling in the air nearby.

It was my hometown, and I loved it. I felt at home here in a way I'd never felt anywhere else.

"So what delayed your return?" Rhys asked, interrupting my mental meandering.

I shrugged, our eyes meeting briefly before we

both looked ahead as we walked. "Just some scheduling challenges with one of our distributors."

"I got your email," he added. "Glad to hear all of that was sorted out with that brewery down there."

Fireweed Industries was much more than a brewery now, but our mainstay was our beer, wine, and mead production. It had started small in our town and grown by leaps and bounds since the generation before our parents had started the business. They got going at a time before handcrafted wines and beers were all the rage. Once they started making money, they expanded, buying up holdings for land, mining, and other projects until a small family business was a large international corporation.

Ever since Rhys had taken over as CEO, one of his goals was to reconnect and focus more on the roots of our corporation. He'd worked to transition any environmentally destructive projects into renewable-focused alternatives. As such, a lot was shifting around. My role as the problem solver for the corporation kept me insanely busy.

Another gust of wind whipped by, and a few snowflakes floated from the sky. I glanced up to the mountains behind our town, commenting, "Termination dust fell last week. With it being almost November, we can expect to get snow down here soon."

Termination dust was mountain speak for the end of autumn when the first snow fell on the mountains.

Rhys murmured his agreement as the sign for Spill the Beans Café came into view. With its shimmery pink lettering and coffee beans spilled underneath, the sign easily stood out in the overcast day. This little café was a favorite local hangout. They were ahead of the game with Christmas decorations and already had festive lights strung up around the windows and on two trees out front.

A moment later, we pushed through the door, and I breathed a sigh of relief at the warmth. Glancing at Rhys, I commented, "Even though I know it's starting to get cold, all I wore was this." I tugged at my light-weight fleece jacket.

Rhys shrugged, glancing down at his own. "We have the same problem. I love winter, but I'm not a huge fan of heavy coats."

We got in line, and I glanced around. The café was cute with wide-plank hardwood flooring, small round wooden tables with chairs scattered about the space, and local artwork hung on the walls. The chalkboard behind the counter at the back had a list of their wide variety of coffee and tea drinks, along with the food menu.

"I see Haven's made some updates," I observed, sliding my gaze to my brother's.

Rhys cast me a grin. "She insists on updating the chalkboard for them whenever they need it. Even though she only fills in here and there now."

Haven Rivers was Rhys's fiancée. They'd also had a baby, a pleasant surprise for them. My brother was happier than I'd ever known him to be since he finally got his head screwed on and realized how much Haven meant to him.

She had her own online business for handmade wedding announcements and so on but had also taken a job working for our public relations department with our sister McKenna who headed that up. Before that, she'd been working here at the café to supplement her income from her online art business and kept the chalkboard menu bright and whimsical.

We were at the counter a moment later, and Hazel

smiled at us. Hazel owned Spill the Beans Café with her best friend, Phyllis. I didn't remember not knowing them, as this café had been around since I'd been a little boy.

"Well, hi there," Hazel said, her warm gaze flicking from Rhys to me. "What can I get you guys today?"

"I'll take a plain coffee, the darkest roast you have," I said.

Rhys chimed in, "Same for me."

Hazel began prepping our coffees, asking, "Anything to eat?"

Just then, a voice came from behind us. "I want something to eat."

Rhys and I glanced back to find Blake there. Blake landed behind Rhys in our line of siblings. Seven of us were left after our eldest brother, Jake, passed away during his senior year in college from alcohol poisoning. Our family had some skeletons in the closet. Although I supposed none of them were secrets because most people knew. Secrets weren't easy to keep in a small town.

"Hey, dude," I said with a grin as Blake cuffed me lightly on the shoulder.

He greeted Hazel and Rhys before pointing out, "You didn't answer Hazel." He gestured toward her.

She chuckled as she handed me my coffee.

"I do want something to eat. Actually, why don't we share one of those new pizzas?" I glanced back and forth between my brothers.

"Sounds good to me. I'm starving," Blake replied.

"Fiona not feeding you well?" I teased.

Fiona was Blake's new love and the chef at the Fireweed Winery restaurant.

Blake ran the production and distribution arm of Fireweed Industries, which was attached to the restaurant. In all honesty, the restaurant was basically a passion project. Oh, it made us money, but it was the smallest part of our business and managed entirely by the prior chef, David.

Blake cracked a grin, his gray eyes twinkling. "Fiona always feeds me well even though I try to make sure she doesn't cook for me too much. But there's a big event today at the winery, so I'm staying out of the fray. It's not locals' night, so it's not my gig."

Rhys and Blake shared the same coloring of dark blond hair and gray eyes, just like my twin brother, Adam. I got my dark hair and blue eyes from my mom. Aside from me and Wyatt, the rest of our siblings all shared the same coloring.

"Pizza works for me," Rhys said.

Hazel handed him his coffee, asking Blake, "Plain house coffee?"

Blake flashed her a grin as he dipped his chin. "Always."

Just then, a teenage guy came out from the back door. Hazel called over. "They want the pizza special today." She looked at us for a beat, her gaze calculating. "I'm going to say they need two large pizzas."

"Of course we do," I quipped. "One large is not enough. That's only eight pieces."

"Just what I thought," Hazel replied with a wink as she handed Blake his coffee.

"Just put that on our tab," Rhys said.

We each stuffed bills into the tip jar as Hazel tapped on the keyboard on the register. She smiled at us. "Boys, you don't all have to tip."

"Yes, we do," Blake returned.

"Especially if you're gonna call us boys," I teased with a wink.

She waved us away when the bell chimed over the

door. I knew before I even looked over my shoulder that Quinn had just entered the café.

"Well, hey there, Quinn," Blake said as he turned to smile at her.

Fuck my life. I would have to play it cool. I'd better figure out how to do that. I wouldn't be able to avoid Quinn without stirring up far more questions than I cared to contemplate.

Turning, I pasted a casual smile on my face as Quinn stopped beside Blake. "Hi, Quinn."

I hoped my voice sounded casual and easy. All the while, every cell in my body started firing, sending little lightning bolts of desire through me.

Her eyes met mine, and I could've sworn sparks sizzled in the air between us. "Hi," she replied.

Her voice sounded husky, but that had to be crazy. I'd heard Quinn's voice almost daily for years. How could I have missed that? Her voice was low and throaty with a raspy edge.

Rhys asked her about some paperwork. I took that opportunity to take a step back, commenting, "I'm going to grab us a table."

I gritted my teeth as I turned away and heard Rhys say, "You should join us for lunch."

Normally, I would've been the one to invite her to sit with us. I told myself I needed to get used to this and that this fiery-hot lust for her would have to fade. It fucking had to.

Blake was right behind me and sat down across for me. "Everything okay?" he prompted after a swallow of his coffee.

Blake was perceptive. Aside from Adam, my twin, he was my closest brother. Personality-wise, we were similar. We liked to joke around and got along easily.

"Of course," I replied, my voice too forceful.

His eyes held mine for another beat before he shrugged, likely observant enough to realize I wasn't about to share my thoughts.

A moment later, Rhys arrived at the table with Quinn. He pulled out the chair beside me for her, and she sat down after a beat of hesitation. He grabbed a chair from a nearby table that was empty after asking the couple seated there. That made our table crowded. Quinn, because she was polite, shifted her chair slightly closer to mine to make room for Rhys's chair.

I took a breath, willing the pounding beat of my pulse to slow the fuck down. She took a swallow of her coffee. My eyes lingered on her mouth. When she lowered her cup, her tongue darted out to slide across her bottom lip, and blood arrowed straight to my cock.

Fuck me. Again. The problem was that I wanted Quinn. Every time I tried to tell myself that it was crazy to want her, another part of me, I supposed the devil of my desire, tried to talk me into why it was a great idea. We were good friends. It didn't have to be anything more.

Yet I wanted more. So much more.

# Chapter Seven

# QUINN

I could literally feel the heat emanating from Kenan. Our thighs were maybe an inch apart at the small table. Every so often, he shifted in his seat, and his knee would brush against mine.

He couldn't be as hyperaware of this as I was. We'd had lunch like this hundreds of times, and sitting close should've elicited nothing. I should not react to him.

I tried to focus on the conversation. Rhys talked about the upcoming opening of a winery and brewery in Willow Brook, Alaska, where one of their cousins lived. With Rhys returning Firewood Industries headquarters to Fireweed Harbor, he focused on expanding the corporation's presence in Alaska and bolstering local communities with employment and business.

"Quinn?" someone prompted. Seeing as I was seated with three of the Cannon brothers and their voices were similar, I wasn't even sure who I hadn't been paying attention to.

I glanced up from my plate. "Yes?"

"I was asking if you knew if the business office had finalized the paperwork for that location," Rhys said.

"Oh yes," I replied quickly. "Everything's taken care of. I think at this point it's in David's lap. He's been coordinating with Archer in Willow Brook. As far as I know, they're getting the place staffed and ready to roll. I'm assuming..." Pausing, I flicked my eyes among the brothers, quickly passing Kenan's gaze. "McKenna will be setting up some kind of event for the opening."

"Oh, she's all over that," Blake said with a grin before he took a bite of pizza. After chewing, he added, "She's been bouncing in and out of the restaurant, checking with Fiona about menu planning and so on. Willow Brook will have a big opening event."

"I'll offer to fly anyone who wants to go down there," Rhys interjected. "Or we can do a ferry trip. It's cold, but it could be fun."

"You should go," Blake said, gesturing toward me.

"Oh, I don't need to go," I said quickly, thinking it was a guarantee that Kenan would be there. Avoiding him when I could, made the most sense at this point.

"Please go," Rhys said firmly. "We'd love it. You work enough as it is, and that'll get you out of your office for a few days."

"Exactly," Kenan said from my side.

Of late, he'd been on my case for working too much. Maybe it was because I was so unsettled or perhaps it was because my panties were drenched with arousal from sitting beside him, but irritation flashed inside. My voice sounded snappy when I replied, "I don't work too much." Blake's gaze met mine, his brow furrowing slightly in concern. I shifted in my seat, striving for a lighter tone. "I like to work, and I enjoy my job."

"And we appreciate everything you do," Rhys said

smoothly. "I'm just saying it would be good for you to go."

I managed to leave soon, making up a fabricated call. I practically ran from the coffee shop back to my office, almost slamming the door behind me and leaning against it.

"What am I going to do?" I whispered out loud.

# Chapter Eight

# KENAN

"I love the idea of a group ferry trip!" McKenna enthused. She looked over at me expectantly.

I managed to nod along. "It's a great idea. Except how do we pull that off?"

"I think we reserve a block of rooms on one of the ferries to Whittier and set up rental cars from there to Willow Brook. The whole family can go, along with some of the staff. People will love it." My sister rested her hands on her hips as she eyed me expectantly.

"Sounds like a plan," I said.

I *did* think it was a great idea. Yet I sensed McKenna was picking up that I was off kilter. I'd felt unsettled and disconcerted ever since that kiss. *That* kiss. Now that Rhys had gone and suggested that Quinn come along on this trip, what was a great idea had me seriously on edge.

McKenna lifted her arms, quickly tightening her ponytail. Her dark blond hair swung as she moved. Her arms fell, and she waggled her brows at me, her gray eyes widening with curiosity. "What's up with you lately?"

"Nothing," I replied quickly.

Clearly too quickly because my sister's eyes narrowed. "Oh, *something* is up."

"Nothing is going on," I ground out.

"Ever since you came back from Seattle, you've just been..." She drummed her fingertips on the counter. "Off."

I briefly contemplated confiding in McKenna but dismissed it as fast as I considered it. McKenna had opinions about *everything*. I loved her, but she would be *all* over this situation with Quinn and me.

"I've just been tired," I finally said. "And, you know, it's that time of year."

Her gaze sobered instantly. "I know." She let out a little sigh.

I was referring to the anniversary of our eldest brother's death. Jake died during his senior year in college from alcohol poisoning at a college holiday party.

We all missed him. I hadn't brought that up just to derail McKenna from wondering about me. Because the day *was* coming, and it always hovered over us as a family. There'd been the tragedy of his death and then the news over two years ago about our grandfather sexually abusing him, a detail our cousin Archer had carried alone for years.

We knew that others from the outside thought our family was lucky. I would never discount the privileges we had from wealth. Even if it was wealth earned through hard work and fairly new, so we weren't assholes and entitled. Most of the town knew that after our father died and our grandparents stepped in to help raise us that our grandfather had been an abusive asshole, verbally and physically, to our oldest brothers. We hadn't known the true depths of the secrets that Jake had carried.

Going through what we did had tightened the bonds between us seven surviving siblings. To this day, we joked about the size of our family. But with two sets of twins, it just worked out that way. Our parents wanted a big family. Here we all were, still close and banged up, but we were stronger for what we'd been through. Our brother Wyatt of the younger set of twins, Wyatt and Griffin, kept himself at a distance. I suspected Griffin knew why and maybe someday the rest of us would find out. With Jake gone, Rhys was the oldest, followed by Blake, then me and my twin, Adam, followed by Wyatt and Griffin, and then McKenna. She might've been the only sister and the youngest, but she was a force of nature. She was strong-willed, bordering on stubborn, opinionated, and super smart.

I loved her to pieces, but I wasn't ready to have her voicing her opinion on Quinn. She'd fallen quiet. We were at the main offices in a break room.

McKenna lifted her eyes from the counter. "We'll always have to remember that," she said. "It makes me tired sometimes."

"Same here." I lifted my glass of water to take a swallow. "We loved him, and we always will."

Blessedly, Blake came walking into the room, smiling over at us. "Hey there." He plunked down in the chair beside where McKenna stood. "Why are you standing?" he asked.

"She likes to pace when she's excited," I quipped, using the interruption to lighten the moment.

McKenna narrowed her eyes but burst out laughing. "It's true."

"What's up?" Blake prompted as he reached for a

spoon on the table and began twirling it between his fingers.

"McKenna's all over this plan for us to do some kind of family and staff ferry trip to Willow Brook for the opening of the new winery and brewery location."

"I think it's a great idea," Blake said firmly.

"It is, and I'm making it happen." McKenna nodded vigorously in emphasis.

Just then, I heard footsteps and knew they were Quinn's. For fuck's sake, I even recognized the pace of her stride.

McKenna turned just as Quinn walked past the doorway. "Quinn!" she called.

Quinn stopped and took a few steps backward, looking through the door. McKenna waved her in. "We're doing it, and you're going for once."

"Going where?" Quinn prompted.

"The group ferry trip to Willow Brook. The one Rhys suggested. We'll take the ferry to Whittier and drive to Willow Brook from there."

"Oh." Quinn's reply was wildly vague.

I took the moment to take her in. She wore fitted jeans tucked into leather boots that rose halfway up her calves. Atop that, she wore a silky cream blouse. Her light brown hair was down today, falling in soft waves around her shoulders. She lifted her hand, pressing the center of her glasses and pushing them up on her nose.

I swallowed, trying to ignore the heat that blazed through me.

"Kenan?" McKenna prompted.

"What?"

"I'm putting you in charge."

"Public relations is your thing," I replied.

"No, in charge of figuring out this ferry situation. Whether we can rent a whole block or something."

"What do you think, Quinn? You'll go, right?" McKenna pressed.

Quinn cleared her throat. "Of course. Sounds great."

My sister's eyes shifted to me, her brows hitching up expectantly. "Of course, I'm going."

McKenna's phone chimed, and only seconds later, she hurried out to take a call. Blake's phone buzzed, and he also moved to leave. "You just got here," I pointed out as he stood.

"I know, but it's Fiona."

That was all he had to say. Blake, who I'd never considered susceptible, was deeply in love with Fiona. He would do anything for her. I waved him out with a grin.

"Quinn'll keep you company," Blake said as he passed by her, cuffing her lightly on the shoulder and winking. "You guys are besties."

Another moment later, it was just Quinn and me. Quinn stood awkwardly beside the table. This should've been an easygoing moment for us. Instead, my neck and shoulders felt tight, and my confused heart started to beat faster in my chest.

I cleared my throat. "We should get coffee," I suggested. My voice sounded strained, even to my own ears.

"Sure. Just text me sometime. I have to go," she said quickly.

She began to turn away, and I stood from the table. "Quinn."

She came to a stop, and I noticed that her shoulders were held stiffly. She clutched a file folder against her chest as she turned around to face me. "Yes?" Her voice was stilted and polite, and I suddenly hated all of this.

"Is everything okay?"

She nodded jerkily. "Sure. You?"

I jammed my hands in my pockets, scuffing my toe lightly across the tiled floor. "Yeah, fine."

She began to turn away again, and I reached for her reflexively. The moment my fingers landed on her elbow, I could feel the reverberation of that touch through my entire system. It was just her elbow, for fuck's sake. I dropped my hand swiftly, as if it had been burned.

"I don't want things to be weird with us," I said.

"They're not weird," she insisted.

Despite my own tension and near constant state of uncertainty around her every time our paths crossed, or I even thought about her, irritation pricked me. I didn't like that she was trying to pretend nothing happened. Because *something* had, something important. I knew I wasn't alone in how I felt. Maybe I didn't know what the hell to do, but I suddenly felt as if I wasn't worth it to her.

It wasn't something I voiced aloud, but, for whatever reason, I tended to feel like the left-out sibling in our family. Rhys was the CEO. Fuck no, I didn't want that job. It was far more responsibility than I cared to deal with. Blake headed up the brewery and winery production. He knew his place. He was made for that. Adam was the numbers guy. He fucking loved being the CFO.

With McKenna being our PR person and Griffin and Wyatt content as hotshot firefighters who stared risk in the face as part of their job, they had a place. No one bothered to consider what I wanted. Yet if they asked, I wouldn't have been able to answer. I was the filler-in when someone needed to step up and do something no one else knew what to do with.

Apparently, even the woman who'd become my closest friend over the past few years didn't think I was worth the trouble.

"Don't try to pretend," I said, my voice coming out low and laced with a hint of my simmering frustration.

Quinn turned to face me fully, her eyes coasting over my face before holding my gaze. Her look was direct, perceptive, and assessing.

"I'm not pretending," she finally said. She lifted her free hand in the air, letting it fall. "I don't know what to do. I don't want to screw up our friendship."

"I don't either." I was relieved she didn't try to sidestep the obvious.

She still didn't look away from me, and I started to feel uncertain, shifting on my feet before scuffing my toe against the floor again. I hated that I felt so unsettled with her now. Not much got to me, but that kiss had. The chasm it had created between us bothered me even more.

"Let's have dinner tonight," I said.

"A date?" she prompted.

I shrugged. I didn't know how to define it. "Look, your friendship is important to me. We've had dinner plenty of times. Let's just talk."

She was quiet, and a subtle flush crested on her cheeks. The desire simmering on low burn whenever I was near her sent sparks leaping inside me.

Her eyes broke away from mine. Her hand clenched on the file folder against her chest. She stared out the window for a moment, and I followed her gaze. With our headquarters smack in the middle of downtown Fireweed Harbor, we had an excellent view of the harbor. Boats bobbed in the water, and the sun was high in the sky, striking sparks on the surface.

She looked back at me. "Okay. Are we going out?"

We often got takeout together and watched shows at her place. "It's pizza night," I pointed out. "I'll bring pizza to your place. Does that work?" I felt my lips curling into a smile. I'd missed my nights with Quinn.

When she smiled back, my heart gave a tricky beat in my chest. "That works. See you at seven."

# QUINN

I rested my hands on the counter in my kitchen, trying to take a calming breath. Ever since I'd agreed that Kenan could come over like he usually did, I'd been an anxious mess. We always watched *Grey's Anatomy* together. We loved getting caught up in the drama.

I released my breath in a gust as I straightened. "This is no big deal," I said to myself.

*Maybe I can forget about that stupid kiss. He's just a friend. You know you could never have anything with him.*

Kenan had told me more than once that he couldn't imagine himself being serious with anyone. He was still shocked that two of his brothers had fallen in love. He'd always said his family's history had taught him love wasn't worth it.

He wasn't a jerk and didn't use people. He played the field in college, but nothing out of the ordinary. Here and there, he dated. He didn't speak of it much, but to this day, I thought he went to Juneau and Seattle for travel on occasion to meet with women who weren't too close for comfort and accepted a no-strings arrangement with him.

I spun my bracelet in a circle on my wrist. I shook my hands consciously and strode from my kitchen down the short hallway to my bathroom. My dog's claws clicked on the floor behind me as she followed.

Bela was a rescue from a hoarding situation. She was a beagle-sheltie mix, and I adored her. She was still a shy girl as she hadn't been socialized at all before she landed with me. She was as loyal as could be and shadowed me everywhere I went, inside and out. She stayed with my parents whenever I was traveling with work, and they spoiled her extra.

I loved my little house. It was mine, just mine. It was a small single-story, modern ranch. A family who vacationed here built it, but then they didn't travel here much, so they sold it. When it was up for sale and I could afford it, I snapped it up quickly.

It had light hardwood flooring and big windows in every room. There were built-in shelves in the hallway and an angled roof that rose high in the front, offering light all through the house, even down the hallway. One side of the hallway was lined with windows and the other with the doorways to bedrooms. I had my own suite with a bathroom that included a luxurious soaking tub and a rainfall shower. There were two other bedrooms, one of which I had turned into an office. I didn't like to admit it, but I was prone to working even when I was at home.

I studied myself in the mirror when I walked into my bathroom. I had changed out of my jeans into a pair of comfortable cotton pants with a wide waistband that rested low on my hips. I wore a ribbed tank top above that with a lightweight cardigan sweater that fell to my hips.

My hair was still down, and I contemplated putting it up in a ponytail. I acted decisively as soon as I thought that, snatching my brush off the counter and swiftly brushing my hair up and back into a ponytail high on top of my head. I pushed my glasses up on my nose.

"Stop worrying about how you look," I ordered myself.

I heard tires on my gravel driveway and dashed out of the bathroom, slowing to a walk as I turned out of my bedroom doorway into the hallway. I didn't want Kenan to see me running down my hallway, so I stopped in a little alcove between the hallway and the living room area. I could see out front from here, but he couldn't see me because there was a built-in shelf on the wall serving as a natural divider between the hallway and the living room.

I watched as Kenan climbed out of his SUV and pulled out the pizza boxes. His vehicle was dark navy, and I'd teased him more than once that it matched his eyes. I watched as he approached my house, his gait long and easy. He had two pizza boxes resting on one arm and clutched two six-packs of beer or something else in his hand.

He knocked lightly, opening the door without waiting. Because those were the kind of friends we were. "Hey there!" he called when he closed the door behind him. I composed my expression and rounded the corner into the living room.

"Hey, hey," I returned and pasted a polite smile on my face.

"I got our usual," he said as he walked across the living room toward the kitchen.

I followed him, stopping beside the counter. It was a wide rectangle island with bright royal-blue tiles.

"One pepperoni and one mushroom?" I prompted as Bela circled Kenan's legs.

He was one of a few people she felt comfortable with beyond me.

He waggled his brows. "Of course. I made sure to get the new holiday mead and some beer."

"Oh. You beat me to that. I haven't been by the winery in a few days. The holiday one is that spiced cider beer and mead, right? I wish they had that all year."

Kenan set the beer and mead on the counter. "Same here. Blake says they don't do that because he likes to charge more money for it."

Fireweed Winery made some of the best wine, beer, and mead around, most definitely in Alaska. They'd won some national awards over the years as well. It was the Cannon family legacy.

Kenan glanced at his watch. "We've only got fifteen minutes until the show starts. Let's get going."

The next hour or so felt mostly normal. Well, except for the fact that Kenan sat near me on my couch, which suddenly seemed ridiculously small. I had what I thought was a generously sized sectional, but the side that faced the television was shorter.

As if he could read my mind, Kenan commented, "You need a bigger couch."

This wasn't the first time he had said as much. I slid my gaze to his, wishing I didn't notice how stunning his eyes were. They were bright, almost starlight blue.

My belly flipped, and I took an unsteady breath. "You've mentioned that," I said, trying to keep my voice light.

"Well, it bears repeating," he said dryly.

There was, maybe, at best, a foot and a half between us on my couch. I could feel the heat radiating from him across that short distance. Or perhaps my body felt like it was on fire being close to him. I'd never quite understood the concept of being hot and bothered by someone until now.

Sweet hell. I was deeply in lust with my friend and didn't know how to make it go away. I didn't want us to be those friends who grew apart, or those friends who ruined a perfectly good friendship with sex. I just wasn't the kind of person who could do casual. It had never gone well for me.

I tried to carefully take a deep breath. With my pulse strumming along, stumbling and tripping with its racing pace, my breath felt short. I worried I would get light-headed due to a lack of oxygen.

Unfortunately, I couldn't quite pull it off. Kenan cocked his head to the side. "Are you okay, Quinn?"

"Uh-huh," I managed, swallowing before taking a gulping breath.

"Were you holding your breath?" His eyes held a sly, teasing gleam that I knew all too well.

"No," I retorted.

Something happened in the show, drawing a noisy laugh from one of the characters.

Kenan's gaze flicked toward the television, much to my relief. He knew me too well. He had to sense that I felt off balance and out of whack. Normally, he would tease me about it. It spoke volumes that he let it drop after asking me if I'd been holding my breath.

I didn't realize my gaze lingered on him until he turned. I was instantly snagged in the intense beam of his eyes.

I swallowed. "What?" I pressed.

I was eager to banter with him, to fall into the comfortable, easy pattern of our friendship where we lightly ribbed each other and tried to one-up each other in conversation. Except my effort was beyond weak.

"I want to kiss you again," he said abruptly.

It was a good thing I was sitting down. If I hadn't been, I would've stumbled and fallen flat on my face. I was *that* shocked at his blunt statement.

"Wha-a-a-a-t?" I sputtered.

"Exactly what I said."

If it had been possible, I didn't doubt flames would've flickered through the air between the line of his gaze and mine. Heat blazed through me. My pulse raced even faster. Butterflies massed in my belly, twirling and sending tingles radiating throughout me.

I was already on the edge of breathlessness, and this tipped me right over. I could hear the pounding rush of blood in my ears with every thundering beat of my heart.

I didn't realize my mouth had dropped open until he lifted his hand, his knuckles nudging just barely under my chin. I snapped it closed and didn't even hide the fact that I had to take a deep, shaky breath.

"What?" I repeated, this time without stumbling over the single-syllable word.

"I said I want to kiss you," he repeated.

It took more effort than I cared to admit, but I tore my gaze away from his. I needed to find some composure. As it was, I felt as if I were scrambling on an icy surface, slipping and losing my balance again and again.

I wanted to kiss Kenan again, more than he could imagine and more than I had ever imagined myself wanting to kiss anyone. Yet I didn't want to ruin our friendship. I knew he didn't believe in love, and I understood why. It wasn't as if I was looking for love. I tried to tell myself maybe I could do this thing, but my doubts were noisy in my thoughts. Because I worried that I would care too much. I worried that I would want too much.

I didn't consider myself a needy woman, the kind of woman who demanded commitment from the very first date. Yet I cared about Kenan as a friend. Deeply. No matter what, I would be dealing with him in my life. The potential ramifications of complications were significant.

I decided my only option was, to be honest. "I don't know if that's such a good idea."

He studied me. "Obviously, it's probably not a good idea," he agreed.

"We're friends first. I don't want this to get in the way," I whispered.

Kenan shifted closer to me, angling to face me. The couch felt much smaller, and I could barely breathe.

"It's already in the way," he said slowly, his voice doing funny things to my insides.

Heat continued to roll through me in slow waves. The memory of how it felt to kiss him was sharp and visceral. Unconsciously, I licked my lips. His eyes darkened.

"Maybe you have a point." My voice was a raspy whisper, and I could barely hear over the pounding beat of my heart.

"We're friends first," he repeated my words back to me. "It'll stay that way. Let's just maybe—"

I couldn't believe what I did, but I cut him off. I made the first move, practically lunging for him. Fiery seconds ticked by when our lips met again. My move had genuinely been a lunge, messy and uncoordinated, and I landed half across his lap. He moved smoothly, shifting me and tugging me into his lap. Once again, I straddled him, just like that night in the hotel. I could feel his arousal underneath me. I could also feel my arousal, slippery wet at the apex of my thighs.

His tongue glided against mine, and I savored the way his hand slid halfway into my hair, and his thumb brushed along the edge of my jaw. His touch was confident and unhurried. Meanwhile, I was near frantic inside, rocking over the hard ridge of his arousal. Once again, I was restless and needy.

We broke apart, our breath coming in ragged heaves as we stared at each other.

# Chapter Ten

# KENAN

Quinn's stunning eyes were dark as they held mine. Her cheeks were pink, and her lips were puffy and swollen from our kiss. I felt, well, there was no other way to put it — wildly out of control inside. Desire pounded in a relentless drumbeat through my body. My cock was so hard it hurt. I knew that later tonight, I would be once again finding my own release with my hand as visions of Quinn danced in my thoughts.

As Quinn stared at me, I tried to shackle my need, to wrestle it under my control. It was a total waste of effort. My heart drummed out a chant of want and need.

I tried to slow my breath, and I succeeded, just barely, taking in at least one deep, steadying breath. "What if —" I began.

She blinked rapidly, looking away and catching her bottom lip with her teeth. I knew that habit of hers. Because I knew her well. I'd often see her in her office, jotting notes with a pencil and biting the corner of her lip when she was thinking. She said she liked to write by hand because it helped her when it came to strategy. As a corporate lawyer, it wasn't that she ended up in court all that much, but she constantly reviewed contracts and made recommendations for us and helped, usually me, handle odd problems.

Although it had never happened before, the sight of her teeth creating a little dent in the smooth pink surface of her lip sent a shot of blood straight to my cock. I had never wanted anyone with such force that I felt a little out of control inside.

"We're friends," she said, almost forcefully.

She was still sitting on my lap. I could feel the heat of her arousal. I had to grit my teeth to keep from rocking my hips into hers.

"We are," I agreed. "We've already kissed," I pointed out.

Quinn rolled her eyes, the pink on her cheeks deepening. "So we have. What's your point?"

"We can't take that back. We've kissed twice. I want you, and you want me, so what would it hurt to see where it goes?"

She studied me quietly. I knew that big brain of hers was spinning through scenarios. She swallowed, blinking and biting the corner of her lip again.

Her chin rose slightly as she stared at me. I felt as if she were daring me to question her even though she hadn't said anything yet.

"What?" I pressed, a familiar feeling rising inside— the urge to spar with her. Hell if I knew why because I sure as fuck didn't know what she was going to say.

"Fine. We can see where this goes. But if it starts getting weird, we agree to stop, and we're friends. Are you clear?" She actually wagged her finger at me.

A sense of triumph rose inside, the feeling pouring into the desire already rushing through me. "Crystal clear," I said slowly. "Anything else?"

"Yeah. We're not having sex."

"Why not?" That question slipped out before I could think better of it.

Quinn's eyes narrowed. "Because I said so."

"So we're just going to kiss and fool around?"

All things considered, that was perfectly fine with me. Well, maybe not perfectly fine. The idea of being buried deep inside Quinn was beyond tempting. But I'd had enough sex to know that plenty of things could be just as good as the full act.

"Yes, we're just going to kiss and fool around," she said, her tone pointed and sharp.

I had one hand resting on her hip and couldn't resist giving her a light squeeze as I replied, "You're fucking hot when you're bossy."

She rolled her eyes.

"I have another question." I held my hand up as if I were a student in a class, Quinn's class.

She pressed her lips together, letting out what I could only describe as a prissy little sigh. "Yes?" Her brows arched up.

"Are we done for the night?"

"Done with what?"

I knew she was flustered, or she wouldn't have quite lost the thread like that. I smiled, my hand sliding up from her hip over the sweet dip at her waist and along her side, resting just where I could feel the curve of her breast on the edge of my thumb.

"Done kissing and fooling around for tonight? I know you like things to be clear, so I just wanted to clarify."

I finally gave in to the urge to nudge my hips upward slightly. I knew there had to be friction. When she let out a startled gasp, it was all I could do not to nudge again.

"I don't know," she rasped, sounding a little breathless. "What do you think?"

"I think I want to make you come, sweetheart."

"Tonight?" she squeaked.

Teasing Quinn like this was *way* too fun. "Yes. Tonight."

"I said no sex," she whispered fiercely.

"I know what you said."

She bit the inside of her cheek as she studied me. "I don't think it's that easy."

"I didn't say it would be easy. I said I wanted to make you come. At least let me try."

# Chapter Eleven

# QUINN

Kenan held my gaze. Although I knew he enjoyed teasing me, I also sensed he was as shocked as I was at the depth of our response to each other. This chemistry that had shimmered to life between us seemed to have its own life force.

I highly doubted Kenan, or any man for that matter, could make me come, with or without sex. Relaxing wasn't easy for me. Tangled up in my insecurities about men, I found that my few sexual encounters had left me deeply unsatisfied.

I knew it was stupid. I knew it was reckless. I *definitely* knew it was foolish. Yet despite all the warnings my brain blared, I couldn't resist. I also didn't want to stop.

I scrambled together a sense of composure to rise to what I knew I needed to do. To not put anything into it. To know that it was just fooling around. I thought I was missing the quality where I wanted to find love and where I wanted someone to fall in love with me.

I remembered being nerdy and awkward in high

school and hating that, but also watching girls and boys flip out over whoever they had a crush on and just not experiencing the same thing. College and law school came along, and I had other priorities. I dated and found sex to be boring. I still kept thinking if I met the right person, that spark would light inside me, but it hadn't happened yet. Of course, it was deeply unsettling and confusing that my friend, with whom I'd never felt anything like this before, elicited the most powerful reaction I'd ever experienced.

For a while, I wondered if maybe women were my thing. But there'd been no spark there either. The passing attraction or chemistry, whatever you want to call it, that I'd experienced on occasion had been enough to make me curious and feel so disappointed. Sex was just a total letdown. My vibrator was way more satisfying and didn't come with any complications.

As my mind spun through these thoughts, Kenan teased his thumb lightly along the side of my breast. My nipples tightened, and I took a shallow breath. My pulse couldn't slow down. It thrummed along in a wild, reckless beat.

"Well?" he prompted.

"Okay," I whispered.

He held my gaze, his eyes darkening as we looked at each other. It almost felt like a fire burning between us, with sparks leaping into the air. Every look, every subtle touch, every sensation was a little rush of air feeding the fire to burn hotter and hotter.

His hand slid to lightly cup my breast, and I almost whimpered. His touch was subtle, his thumb just brushing across the taut, aching peak.

"Is this okay?" he whispered huskily.

I nodded, not even trusting myself to speak. Hell,

if I were honest with myself, I couldn't talk. It was a good thing I was sitting on his lap. My body felt like liquid. I was well beyond weak-kneed and desperate for him.

On the heels of another breath, his lips met mine, and our kiss went wild again. Of course, Kenan just *had* to be an amazing kisser. I felt like everything he did stoked my need higher and higher. With our tongues tangling together and his hips nudging lightly into mine, I once again rocked desperately over him, feeling these little sharp pangs of pleasure at my core. I thought it would be impossible for him to make me come, yet in the back of my mind, the only part that could barely think was stunned. Because I was *soooo* close to my release.

We were fully clothed. Nothing had been bared, yet I wanted to rip everything off and plaster myself to him. At some point, we broke apart, both frantic for air. I felt a sliver of relief at seeing the wild, stunned look in Kenan's eyes.

I wore my comfortable home clothes. The waistband of my cotton pants was resting low on my hips. I felt his hand slide under the hem of my tank top. My skin felt prickly. Everything fed into my frantic desire for him.

"I just need to touch you," he whispered before his lips landed on the side of my neck.

I arched into him like a cat purring, letting out a needy little whimper. "Please," I said.

I didn't even recognize myself. No man had ever even made me contemplate begging. It seemed ridiculous. Yet here I was, begging Kenan to touch me.

He growled against the side of my neck when I felt his palm cup my breast. My breast felt needy, my nipples practically crying out for his touch. He muttered something before lightly squeezing my nipple between his thumb and forefinger. This sent a gush of arousal to my core. My panties were drenched. I was dripping. For him. For Kenan.

He lifted his head, and his eyes dipped down as his palm slid over the soft curve of my belly. "You can tell me to stop at any time."

As if there was any fucking chance of that.

"Don't you dare. I need—" I bit out as his touch shifted into my panties, and his fingers teased into my slippery wet folds.

"Oh fuck, Quinn," Kenan said, his voice almost slurred.

I bit my lip. I was *that* close to coming right now.

"Can I put my fingers inside you?"

We were still staring at each other. I nodded, desperate for his touch inside me.

Slowly, oh-so very slowly, he slid two fingers in me deeply, just as he teased his thumb over my clit. I came instantly, crying out and feeling my channel clenching around his fingers.

We stared at each other, both of us in shock.

# Chapter Twelve

# KENAN

My heart beat so hard and fast that my entire body felt the subtle aftershocks of each resounding kick against my ribs. Somehow, hell if I know how, Quinn and I disentangled ourselves.

I slid my gaze sideways a few minutes later. She sat where she would normally be seated on the couch with the bowl of popcorn on her lap, but she wasn't eating any of it. Her eyes were trained on the television. Her cheeks were still tinged pink, and I could feel the buzz of desire humming through me.

I wanted to reach over, knock that bowl of popcorn on the floor, and pull her back onto my lap. I wanted to kiss her senseless all over again. Only this time, I wanted to make her come all over my cock.

Instead, I yanked my eyes away, staring blindly at the television. I took a slow and quiet breath, willing my heartbeat to slow and willing the desire, practically kicking and screaming inside, to calm the fuck down.

If I thought kissing her was a mistake, this was far worse. I didn't know how to shake it. I didn't know how to back out of it now. Quinn had laid down the marker. It was her call.

Maybe it was habit, perhaps it was because we'd known each other for so long, or maybe it was because there was no other choice, but somehow, we dragged ourselves back onto familiar ground. We laughed at an episode of a sitcom. I think maybe I ate four pieces of popcorn to Quinn's single piece.

When the show finished, I slid my palms down my thighs, saying, "I gotta roll," as I stood from the couch, something I said every week.

Quinn went to bed early. She always had. Or so she told me. She said she liked to get to the office before other people so she could have some quiet time to work before dealing with too many interruptions.

She walked me to the door, as she usually did. When I glanced down, it was as if a rubber band snapped back into place. I wanted to kiss her all over again.

She looked up at me, blinking twice. "Well," she said, her voice bright and a little strained.

*Don't kiss her again*, my rational mind said.

*But I want to. We've already gone this far. What's the sense in stopping now?*

*Points for logic*, my rational mind offered, dry tone, and all.

*Fuck it.*

As I held her gaze and saw the heat still flickering there, mingling with hints of my uncertainty, I thought it made the most sense to kiss her again.

At least then, we could stop worrying. At least then, the need and desire would get a tiny release valve.

"Good night," she whispered, seeming to have given up on trying to be forced and bright.

I took a step, looking down as I lifted a hand to nudge her chin up with my knuckles.

"Good night," I rasped.

The shape of my words moved against her lips before I gave her a lingering kiss. For a split second, I thought she might pull away, but she didn't. She let out this soft little sigh and the barest hint of a whimper in the back of her throat as her mouth opened underneath mine.

A few minutes later, I was driving home, my cock aching. What the fuck did I just do?

# Chapter Thirteen

# QUINN

The only reason I got any sleep was because I gave in and had a moment with my trusty vibrator. I should've already been sated since I'd had an explosive climax with Kenan. Yet then he'd gone and kissed me before he left, leaving my body in a jumble of restless need.

As it was, I'd clocked, at best, four hours of sleep when I finally dragged myself out of bed. It wasn't like I would be able to sleep late anyway. The moment my eyes had opened at five o'clock, I jolted wide awake.

I raced through a shower, studying myself in the mirror as I brushed my hair. I couldn't imagine Kenan really being attracted to me. Although I knew I wasn't the girl I'd been in high school with an unfortunate burst of acne during my sophomore year, I wasn't a stunner by any stretch. I had light brown hair, nothing special. I couldn't wear contacts because I had astigmatism in both eyes, so glasses it was. Although I did like to have a little fun with those. Today, I went with a bright-blue cat-shaped pair.

I spun away from the mirror. I didn't have time to dwell on how I looked. I glanced out the window to see a little bit of snow had fallen the night before. I slipped into a pair of fitted jeans and leather boots with practical soles and pulled on a fitted turtleneck sweater. I needed something to shield me somehow.

When I parked behind the office for Fireweed Industries, I decided to walk over to Spill the Beans Café for some coffee. I needed the caffeine and could use a few minutes of conversation to knock me out of the hamster wheel of my thoughts this morning. Kissing Kenan once had been a blunder. Twice had been an even bigger slipup. Three times? Epically big mistake.

Now, I knew what it felt like to let go with him.

"Stupid, stupid, stupid," I muttered under my breath as I walked down the sidewalk.

"What in the world are you calling stupid?" a voice asked sharply.

Glancing up, I saw Phyllis Lane. Phyllis owned Spill the Beans Café with her best friend, Hazel, who was also curious and opinionated.

I blinked and pasted a smile on my face. "Just the slippery sidewalk," I lied as I gestured toward the thin layer of snow coating the sidewalk.

Only one street in Fireweed Harbor had a sidewalk, and we were on it. It *was* slick.

As her perceptive blue gaze studied me, I sensed she knew I was lying, but she was kind enough to let it slide. She nodded. "That stupid sidewalk." Her eyes twinkled as she smiled at me. "Where are you headed?"

"Your coffee shop. You?"

She glanced behind her, her gaze bemused when she turned back to me. "Well, I live there, so I was just coming out." She thumbed over her shoulder.

I bit the insides of my cheeks to keep from laughing. "So you do. Shall we walk together then?"

Her smile widened. "Absolutely."

I looked around as we walked down the street. I loved my little hometown. I'd felt lucky to grow up in Fireweed Harbor. The picturesque town was tucked into the base of the mountains beside the sparkling waters of the Inside Passage. Not many places in the world had such startling and breathtaking beauty. With the mountains reaching high into the sky, a glacier glowing blue under the early morning sunshine, evergreens flanking the mountains, and snow topping off the tall peaks and the ocean right there, glittering from where the sun shimmered on the surface, it was postcard-worthy. Even though the town was small, and sometimes it felt like everyone knew everyone's business, it was home for me.

Some people grew up wanting to spread their wings and fly away. I wanted to see more than this pretty corner of Southeast Alaska, but I always knew I wanted to return home. I'd gone to college in Juneau and law school in the lower 48, the term Alaskans used to describe the continental United States.

When my parents asked if I wanted to take a position in the family law firm, the eventual answer had been a foregone conclusion. Yet I'd wanted to sharpen my skills elsewhere at first. I worked in two different law firms in Seattle before coming home. Sometimes I thought I had been just biding my time, but I genuinely felt it had been important to see how things were outside the small world of Fireweed Harbor. Although Fireweed Industries was a major corporation, it was family-owned. My family's law firm had handled legal work for them for decades.

"Quinn?" Phyllis's voice kicked me off my meandering train of thought about Fireweed Harbor and my law career, bringing me back to this very moment.

She nudged me with her elbow. When I glanced down, her sharp gaze met mine. "Your thoughts sure can wander. We're here."

I'd almost walked by. Spill the Beans Café was immediately to our left. The cute little sign with its shimmery pink lettering and coffee beans spilled underneath already had Christmas lights encircling it.

Phyllis slipped her hand through my elbow, tugging me off the sidewalk onto the walkway. "How did we do?" she asked.

"With what?"

She stopped and gestured with her hand toward two blue spruce trees in the small lawn in front of the café, decorated with holiday lights and red bows.

"They look great," I said with a nod. "You all always do a good job."

The lights on the trees were somewhat haphazard but festive. The small porch in the front where customers enjoyed their coffee and food in the warmer months had lights strung up above and dangling down. Instead of a wreath, a cluster of sleigh bells had spruce tied around it with a big red velvet bow mounted to the door.

The bells jingled as we opened it, heralding our arrival. Warmth enveloped us as we entered, with the almost-winter air following us into the café in a swirl. Phyllis let out a satisfied sigh as she squeezed my elbow before sliding her arm out.

I stopped at the back of the line, and she looked up at me. "Are you okay?" she asked.

It was early yet, and a few customers were over in the corner, but Hazel was busy talking quietly with the one customer in front of us, so we had a moment of privacy.

I considered her question before nodding. "I am. Sometimes life gets me overthinking."

Her perceptive gaze held mine as her lips curled into an understanding smile. "That it does. Thinking too much really is like chasing your tail. If you had one, that is."

With that, she winked and hurried behind the counter, pushing through the waist-high swinging door into the back. When I got to the counter, Hazel beamed when she saw me. "Good morning, Quinn. I always love seeing you."

"The feeling's mutual," I said lightly.

As she prepped my coffee a moment later, she asked, "Do you want anything to eat?"

Just then, the door opened with another gust of winter air blowing in. I reflexively glanced back to see Tessa Hensen walking in with Fiona and Blake Cannon. I smiled at them before replying, "I'll take one of those orange cranberry muffins."

Tessa stopped beside me. "Hey there, Quinn. I'm assuming you're like me. You're here early because you're going to work early."

"You know it," I returned as I stepped to the side.

"I always feel smarter when I see you," she added.

"Smarter?" I prompted

She smiled. "Absolutely. You were the smartest girl in our class. Valedictorian and everything."

Fiona, who was newer to town, glanced over, her brows rising. "Wow."

I shifted my shoulders before shrugging. "Not really. I was a rule follower. Research shows that valedictorians actually don't end up being the most successful in life. We're just good at following rules and doing what we think others want."

Tessa's eyes narrowed. "You're smart as hell, and you should be proud of that."

Blake grinned over at me. "You should. You raise the bar for everyone. One of these days, you'll rub off on Kenan."

Blake's comment elicited a surge of protectiveness for Kenan. He was loyal, bright, and creative. Even though he never spoke of it, I sensed he often felt lost in the shuffle of his crowded family. "Kenan doesn't need me to rub off on him. What would you guys do without him? Whenever you have some weird, complicated situation and need someone to straighten it out, he's your guy."

Blake's brows rose as he nodded. "True."

They were busy ordering when the door to the café opened again. This time, Adam and Kenan came walking in. Even though they were twins, they were fraternal, so they weren't identical. Their features were similar, although Kenan had dark hair and blue eyes to Adam's dark blond hair and slate gray eyes.

The mere sight of Kenan sent a jolt of visceral electricity through me. Heat struck me in a wave, blasting me from head to toe. My pulse shot into the stratosphere, racing so fast my breath felt short instantly.

"Quinn?" Tessa's voice snapped my attention away from Kenan. I hadn't even realized I'd been staring in his direction.

"Yeah?" I brought my attention to her as we stepped to the side together.

"I was just saying we should get together for dinner soon."

"How about tonight?" I asked quickly.

I was desperate not to think about Kenan, and that

would give me something to do other than obsess over him.

Tessa nodded. "Sure. I'll text Haven."

"Rosie, too," I added.

Because I worked a lot, I wasn't the most social person, but I did get together with them on occasion. They were kind of a trio, or had been in high school. I'd gradually been getting more friendly with them since we'd all ended up back in town.

"Let's meet at the winery. I think it's locals' night. Right?" Tessa called over to Blake, who was just stepping to the side after paying for his order.

"Right what?" he prompted as he and Fiona stopped beside us.

"It's locals' night tonight, the weekly tasting," Tessa prompted.

"Sure is," he replied.

"Great. We'll be there. Are you guys going?" Tessa called over to Adam and Kenan.

I resisted the urge to groan. It would be really weird if I tried to say we shouldn't go to locals' night at the winery. I'd gone to the weekly tastings with Kenan countless times.

His eyes landed on mine as Adam replied, "Of course."

I was beyond relieved when Hazel handed over my muffin and coffee. "I need to get going. I've got a few calls to make and some paperwork to take care of early."

"Meet you there tonight," Tessa said as I hurried away.

I practically ran out of the café, relieved for the cold air. I almost unzipped my coat. That's how hot I was inside.

# Chapter Fourteen

# QUINN

A few minutes later, I walked into my office at Fireweed Industries. My office was at the end of the hall upstairs, tucked into a quiet corner. I closed the door firmly. After I stripped out of my coat and tossed it on the back of my chair, I sat down at my desk. My hands shook with nerves. I leaned back in my chair and let out a shaky sigh.

"What the hell am I going to do?" I whispered.

I spun in my chair to look outside. All of the offices had windows facing downtown Fireweed Harbor. The sun rose higher in the sky, and the pink from the sunrise faded to a subtle wash with the orange softening to peach.

I took a slow breath and lifted my coffee off my desk to take a healthy swallow.

"Oh hell," I whispered as I lowered the cup.

I would have to tell Kenan this thing with us had to stop. Because it was crazy. I didn't fancy myself falling for him, but I feared I could, and I really didn't want to screw up our friendship.

Just when I thought I had escaped my dosage of

awkward for the day, I heard a light knock on my office door. Not many people showed up here this early, so my guess was it was Rhys.

"Yes?" I called.

I collected my composure, gathering the tattered ends and bracing myself for whoever walked in. When Kenan peered around the edge of the door, my stomach swooped. "Oh!"

"Mind if I come in?" he asked as he opened the door wider.

It wasn't as if I hadn't known Kenan was handsome before. I took the moment to study him as I nodded. He was tall with broad shoulders. His hair was still damp from what I presumed was a recent shower. His blue eyes were bright.

He closed the door behind him. It wasn't as if he never stopped by my office early in the morning. On occasion, he did because we were friends. Good friends. I tried to ignore the sneaky uncertainty unspooling inside me.

He sat down across from my desk like he usually would. He took a swallow of his coffee while I tried to order my hormones to calm the fuck down. They were ignoring me. My pulse rioted, butterflies tickled the inside of my belly, my breath was short, and heat shimmered through me.

"Good morning," I said, my voice sounding bright and kind of weirdly cheerful to my ears.

"Good morning." His voice was a little low and raspy, and my belly flipped again and again.

We sat in silence for a moment, and I tucked my hands under my thighs because they were shaking again.

"We need to stop," I blurted out.

He leaned forward in his chair, his gaze intent. "Why?"

"Kenan." At first, all I could manage was his name. When he simply waited, I took a slow breath. "You know it's not a good idea."

"I think we've already crossed the threshold of bad ideas," he pointed out. "What if I want more?"

"What?!" I sputtered.

For the first time since he walked in my office, he looked uncertain. He also looked resolved. His usual light, casual, and teasing manner was gone. He studied me quietly before I took an audible breath, letting it out in a sharp sigh.

"Maybe we've already screwed it up, but you're one of my closest friends, and there's something else there." He paused again. I could barely breathe as my heart fluttered madly in my chest. "Let's just see what happens."

"I don't understand," I finally said, genuinely confused.

"I like you, and I'm pretty sure you like me. You say we're friends and—"

"We *are* friends!" My voice came out forceful, almost insistent.

"Did it feel good?" His voice was low.

Butterflies twirled in my belly, and my breath was short. "What do you mean?" I hedged, knowing perfectly well what he meant.

"Kissing me."

My mouth almost dropped open. I crossed my legs, trying to ignore the arousal slick between my thighs.

"You came, sweetheart," Kenan said, his words slow and deliberate.

I snapped my mouth shut, pressing my lips together as I narrowed my eyes. I wanted to lie, to play it off like it hadn't been the best orgasm I'd ever had.

"You know it felt good," I ground out.

His eyes flashed with something like satisfaction. "I won't rush you. But think about what I said. Next weekend is the trip to Willow Brook. We'll be spending the night on the ferry."

Just then, another knock sounded on my office door. Beyond flustered, I called out, "Come on in!"

Adam came striding in. "Surprised to see you here," he teased Kenan as he stopped beside his chair.

Kenan stood. "I was just leaving. What's up with you?"

"Just touching base with Quinn on that tax issue we heard about from one of our producers."

"Well, I'll leave you guys to that," Kenan said.

I didn't even notice I hadn't said goodbye to Kenan until he left the office and Adam prompted, "Everything okay with you two?"

"Oh yeah. Just distracted this morning."

I took a swallow of my coffee, forcing my brain to focus.

# Chapter Fifteen

# KENAN

"Do you think you can handle that?" Adam asked.

"Of course," I replied.

Blake drummed his fingertips on the table where we sat in one of the smaller brewing rooms in the winery and brewery production area. This was the flagship location for the corporation, back where it all began. This warehouse was attached to the restaurant. It was a town favorite and always busy. Despite its local popularity, it only brought in a small drop of the income for our family's business.

"I'll take care of it when we go to Willow Brook next week," I added. "Any updates from David on that end, or Archer?" I glanced at Blake.

David managed the restaurant end of things here after recently stepping down from being our longtime chef. Fiona had taken over as chef and was doing a phenomenal job.

We discussed the planned opening of another brewery, winery, and restaurant location in Willow Brook, where Fireweed Industries had recently opened a renewable energy business in collaboration with another business in Alaska. That was all being run by our cousin, Archer, and half-brother, Chase, in Willow Brook, while David helped with the organization side of things.

"Smooth sailing," Blake replied. "Except for this permit issue."

"Which isn't related to that," Adam chimed in.

The issue in question was a minor land dispute related to a mine Fireweed Industries used to run but had since closed down. We wanted to return the land to a local tribe, and another business was disputing it. Not because they had any claim but because they wanted the land.

"I'm sure Quinn has tidied up all of the legal loose ends," I said with confidence.

"Always. We just want to be present at the meeting to support the tribe," Adam said as he shook his head. "It's not a good look when companies try to take over things like that."

"Yeah, well, I don't think they really care about how it looks," I offered.

"Speaking of Quinn," Adam commented, "is she doing okay?"

I ignored the subtle twist of uncertainty in my chest. "Yeah, why do you ask?"

My twin shrugged. "Not sure. She just seemed a little..." He cocked his head to the side, pressing his tongue into his cheek. "Off today, I guess, when I saw her."

"Oh," I said, keeping my tone casual. "Maybe there's something going on I don't know about."

"Dude, you and Quinn are besties," Blake interjected. "Don't you know everything?"

I felt a low rise of heat inside. For fuck's sake, I

couldn't even think about Quinn without a visceral reminder of our recent encounters.

"I don't know everything. We're good friends, but..." I shrugged. "That still doesn't mean I know everything." I looked toward Adam. "You're my twin brother. I don't assume I know everything about you."

"Pretty sure you do." Adam chuckled.

I rolled my eyes. "Fair enough. You pretty much know everything about me."

Blake grinned at us. "I can't imagine what it's like to be a twin even though I have two sets of twin brothers. I don't know if I'd want to feel like somebody knew everything," he pointed out.

"It's not quite like that," Adam replied. "It's not about the details. It's a vibe thing." He glanced at me. "You know what I mean?"

"Definitely."

Blake opened his mouth to reply when one of the brewers appeared in the doorway. "Blake, you got a sec?"

He stood quickly. "Sure do. Catch you guys later," he tossed over his shoulder as he left the room.

Adam was looking at me when I turned back. "What?" I asked.

"Speaking of that vibe thing, my gut tells me something's up with you and Quinn."

I wanted to deny it, but Adam would sense I was lying. Resting my elbows on the table, I let out a heartfelt sigh. "I kissed her. More than once." I didn't need to share *all* of the details.

Adam looked genuinely surprised, his brows hitching up. "Well, damn. Wasn't expecting you to say that. I told you a few years ago that I thought you two would make a great couple. You said no way, no how, never, that there was zero chemistry," he pointed out as he shook his head slowly. "What changed?"

I ran a hand through my hair. "I was being honest when I said there was no chemistry then. That seems to have changed, and now I don't know what the fuck to do."

"I think you need to tread carefully if you don't want to blow up your friendship."

"I know," I muttered as I leaned back in my chair.

"What do you want?"

"You not to say a fucking thing to anyone about this," I offered dryly.

"You know you don't have to worry about that," he replied, his gaze serious.

"I know." I trusted Adam completely. He had my back, and I had his. Always.

"What do you want?" he repeated, his tone more pointed this time.

"I like her, but I don't think she trusts the situation."

"Of course you like her. That's why you're such good friends."

"Thanks, Captain Obvious," I replied dryly.

Adam chuckled, but he didn't take the bait. After a beat, he added, "It is obvious. I don't think you want to break her heart. I've never known Quinn to really date anyone, at least not locally," he pointed out.

"She doesn't. She doesn't believe in love either. We have that in common."

"Well, I guess you're perfect for each other then. Just let me know when to be ready for the wedding," he quipped.

I let out a ragged sigh. "What should I do?"

Adam studied me for a long moment. Aside from the fact that I trusted him completely, Adam believed in love. He had a girlfriend in college who he loved. She died. He hadn't dated anyone since.

Adam and I were different in many ways but shared the same values. Loyalty meant everything. Maybe I didn't believe in love for me, but I believed in it for him.

"If it's just a few kisses, you can pull back from the brink. But if you actually let it go further, it might get complicated, and then you'll have to deal with that. I can't tell you what to do. I've always thought if you were going to be with anyone, it would be Quinn."

"Seriously?" I pressed.

He nodded, his gaze holding mine so earnestly that my chest tightened.

———

Quinn laughed at something Rosie said. She lifted her beer bottle, and my eyes watched as her lips closed around the opening, and she tilted her head back.

I'd been bound up and tight with need ever since I arrived here tonight and saw her. Her hair was down, falling in loose waves around her shoulders. She wore a pair of fitted jeans tucked into knee-high leather boots with a ribbed cotton camisole that stretched across her breasts and an open button-down flannel shirt over that. All I could think about was how to get her alone to kiss her again.

McKenna appeared at my side. "I don't know if you talked to Tish, but we're sending you and Quinn a day ahead on the ferry."

"If we need to go early, we can fly," I pointed out.

McKenna wrinkled her nose. "Tish already made the reservations, so I just told her to change your date.

I hope that's okay." Her gaze landed on Quinn. "Quinn!" she called.

Quinn had just lowered her bottle of beer. I knew this because I'd pretty much been watching her the whole time. She stepped away from Rosie and approached McKenna and me. "What's up?"

"I was just letting Kenan know you two are going together a day early. You have a meeting with, uh—" McKenna circled her hand in the air.

"On that land issue," Quinn supplied helpfully. "That's fine. Kenan and I will make it fun."

McKenna smiled, letting out a happy little sigh. "Good. So you leave in two days."

McKenna was drawn away into a conversation with Fiona and Haven, leaving Quinn standing with me. We were surrounded by people. I glanced around, my gaze landing on the corner of the bar where Quinn had been sitting when that bolt of lightning struck from the sky, shifting our platonic friendship.

When I glanced back to Quinn, her cheeks were pink.

"That gives you one more day," I said.

"One more day for what?"

"To decide what you want."

I couldn't be logical about her, not anymore.

# Chapter Sixteen

# QUINN

Resting my elbows on the railing, I looked out over the ocean. A light breeze ruffled the water, and the sun was high in the clear blue sky. It was a beautiful day and freezing cold. There was winter in Alaska—or technically pending winter as we hadn't yet reached winter solstice—and then there was winter when you were out on the ocean. It was bracingly cold, and I shivered as I straightened and tucked my hands into the pocket of my down jacket.

"Should we place bets?" Kenan's voice reached me.

Glancing over my shoulder, I saw him approaching from the covered area of the ferry. This wasn't our first ferry trip together. I couldn't recall exactly when, but before his father had died, our families had taken a few trips together on the ferry. One trip was to Kodiak Island, where we saw the massive famed Kodiak brown bears. Back then, Kenan had teased me when my mouth dropped open at the size of the bears, even from a distance.

Over the years, we'd casually kept a tally of what wildlife we might see. Moose weren't included because they were far too common in Alaska. Ferry trips weren't so common. I wasn't even sure I'd taken one with him since we were adults.

"Seagull?" I teased as he stopped beside me.

On cue, a seagull called raucously nearby. Kenan and I turned and glanced behind us, watching as the ferry pulled farther away from Fireweed Harbor. Our cute hometown was becoming distant. We could see the boats bobbing in the harbor and the streets winding up along the hillside into the foothills of the mountains.

I turned forward again, looking ahead. The ferry would stay within view of the shoreline for the first part of this trip. We stopped in Haines before the ferry would approach Southcentral Alaska, where we would dock in Whittier. McKenna had sent Kenan and me a joint email with the itinerary. She had rented us a car there.

With a number of employees from Fireweed Industries, primarily the winery, coming to this opening, she had reserved a block of rooms at a local lodge in Willow Brook where we would all be staying. Kenan and I had rooms side by side. I'd resisted the urge to ask Tish to move my room away from his because that would only send up the smoke signal of gossip about us.

"We might see a humpback," he commented. "And orcas. And what are those little porpoises, the fastest ones in the world?" he prompted.

"Dall's porpoises," I replied.

"Oh, right. I'm sure we'll also see some seals and otters when we dock in Haines. I'd love to see some sea lions basking in the sun. How about a salmon shark?" he asked.

"We could see some Sitka deer in the foothills. Do we count those?" I asked.

"Absolutely. Only moose are off-limits. There are just too many of them," Kenan said firmly.

My lips curled into a smile. We were teasing, but this felt like our usual easy interactions. My heart gave a tricky beat in my chest, stumbling and almost tripping. When I glanced up at him, my belly felt funny, and tingles radiated outward. I knew he'd been teasing a little the other day when he told me I had until this trip to decide what I wanted with us. I knew I could tell him I didn't know, and he would respect that.

Yet I wanted him. No matter how crazy it was—how stupid, foolish, reckless, and more—I also knew I wanted to see where things could go for us.

Feathering along the edges of my thoughts whenever I contemplated this, which was just about every spare moment I had, was the reality that I had an appointment coming up soon and was planning to start treatments for IVF.

I hadn't told anyone about this—other than my doctor, of course. I told myself it was no one's business. My mother was fretting and wanted grandchildren. My older brother was an engineer in Diamond Creek, Alaska. He had taken a position as a consultant for the Fireweed Industries venture in Willow Brook, although he would remain in Diamond Creek, because he loved it there.

Meanwhile, my mother was worried because she feared she would never have any grandchildren. I didn't even know how she would feel if I told her my plans around IVF. I hoped she would be thrilled.

"Quinn?" Kenan prompted.

I glanced up. "Yeah?"

"What are you thinking about?"

He nudged me with his elbow in a familiar gesture that usually meant he was teasing. It was nothing much. Yet every touch from him, even that glancing touch, sent my belly into a little flip.

I shrugged, not about to tell him I was thinking about IVF treatments. "Nothing."

A bracing gust of wind blew across the deck, making me shiver slightly. "Let's go in," he said, sliding an arm around my shoulders and steering me toward the covered area of the ferry.

The Alaskan ferry system was beloved. It ferried locals and visitors all up and down the coastline. There were different ferries, but they were all similar. There was an exposed open area on two levels, another outside covered area, and an inside space. This ferry had a movie theater, small cabins, and a cafeteria-style eatery with three meals served daily and snacks available.

In the summer, people could set up tents out on the open deck and under the covered area. They even had heat lamps above.

Just getting out from the wind was a relief. I didn't know what to think about how I felt with Kenan's arm curled over my shoulders. Even before our kisses and more, he had put his arm around my shoulders plenty of times. I just never thought much of it beyond a friendly gesture.

Now, I savored the feel of it and the sense of being sheltered and protected. He kept walking, coaxing me through a doorway leading into an open dining area by the cafeteria with booths lining the windows.

"Want some hot cocoa?" he asked, waggling his eyebrows.

"I'd love some."

"You grab a booth, and I'll get two mugs for us."

His arm fell away from my shoulders, and I instantly missed the feel of his touch.

*"You're being ridiculous,"* I chided myself.

With a mental shake, I scanned the available booths, selecting one toward the center with a good view of the shoreline. Kenan arrived only moments later, handing me one of the cups. The hot cocoa came from one of those automated machines. It wasn't amazing, but it was pretty good and all part of the ferry experience. I remembered loving these ferry rides with my parents and brother when I was younger. They were distinctly an Alaskan experience.

Kenan sat across from me, one of his knees bumping mine as he slipped into the booth. The subtle, brushing touch sent a jolt of electricity spinning through my body. I curled my hands around the warm paper cup before lifting it and taking a swallow. The rich, chocolatey flavor slid across my tongue. Lowering the cup, I said, "Perfect. Thank you."

"Of course."

"Do you know what time we dock in Haines?" I asked.

Kenan shifted to the side slightly to reach down and get his phone out of the pocket of his jeans. His calf bumped mine, and his foot slid between mine. He left it there as he lifted his phone. It was nothing, I told myself. Yet it felt intimate and affectionate to have his foot between mine.

He tapped on his screen. "I saved the schedule." A second later, he added, "In two hours, there's a movie tonight. Are we going?"

"If you want to, I'm game."

"It's the whole experience, Quinn. We've gotta do the movie." He leaned forward with a grin.

I laughed. "Let's do it."

We fell into silence as we sipped our hot cocoa and were looking out the windows when an announcement came over the speakers from the captain. "For your information, a school of Dall's porpoises is swimming nearby. They're the fastest porpoises in the world. You can see them out on the main deck."

"Let's go." Kenan waggled his brows.

We hurried toward the deck along with some other passengers. Watching over the edge of the railing, we enjoyed the view of the tiny porpoises as they zipped through the water, curling over the surface and diving down as they zoomed alongside the front of the ferry.

I glanced at Kenan, feeling a rush of joy. I loved seeing wildlife of any kind. I knew he did too. When he smiled down at me, my heart flipped in my chest.

Only moments later, the porpoises zoomed out of view, and we returned inside to reclaim the same booth. "Have you seen those before?" I asked once we were seated again.

"I'm not sure," he replied. "Maybe when we were kids. Definitely not on any of our regular fishing trips. What about you?"

"I'm not sure either. Maybe on one of the ferry trips with my parents and brother when I was younger."

"On a more serious note," he began a moment later. "Any concerns about this situation with the land?"

I shook my head. "None at all. Legally, we're in the clear." I shrugged. "It's just another business being greedy. It's not as if Fireweed Industries didn't do similar things before, especially earlier on. But we currently own the land, and we're giving it back to the tribe. That's the way it is. This meeting is just a formality. They filed in court, and it didn't go anywhere, so they're trying to negotiate something else. We're not going for it."

Kenan cocked his head to the side, studying me for a few beats. "You kick ass," he said after a long moment.

"I don't recall kicking any asses," I teased lightly.

"You're always the smartest person in the room. You have your shit together, and you kick ass at your job. I like that about you."

His eyes twinkled with his grin, and my heart gave another tricky beat. "You kick ass too," I returned with a firm nod.

"I don't recall kicking any asses lately," he lobbed right back at me.

"You do, and you know it."

His gaze sobered a little, and he shrugged. "Maybe."

I nudged one of my knees against his. "You do. I know you don't always believe it, but you do. You play it off like you're not the smartest in the family. Maybe Adam's a genius with numbers, but you're just as smart as he is. You're also flexible. That's why you're a fixer."

"You make it sound like I'm in the mob," he teased

I rolled my eyes. "You know what I mean."

# KENAN

*You know what I mean.*

Quinn's words repeated in my thoughts. Reminding me, yet again, why she was such a good friend. It wasn't as if I contemplated it often, but I knew she respected me. I knew she didn't dismiss me. Not that I thought others did. But somehow, I tended to feel as if I slipped unnoticed between the cracks in my family.

I loved being a part of a big family because you never felt alone, yet our family could be defining. I would never complain about the privilege I had. We were financially very comfortable. Even though I could tell myself it was because our family worked hard, which was true, it was still a privilege, and there were a few strokes of luck to it. Our world tended to forget that detail. Oh sure, people did work hard, but timing and opportunity didn't always strike. Those factors had worked out for our family.

While I loved being a part of a messy bunch of siblings, we carried our own share of trauma and skele-tons in the closet, some of them more public than others. My mind spun to our great-uncle, who had recently been sentenced for embezzlement.

He was old enough that it would hurt for him to spend time in jail. But it was nothing compared to the crimes he should be paying for, the emotional abuse, the verbal abuse, the casual slaps against some of us, and the sexual abuse of our oldest brother, who'd likely drank himself to death as a result of that trauma.

Jake had chased after the numbness of losing himself in a haze of alcohol. It was a bitter twist, knowing that our family's initial fortune had been built from the winery and brewery, which we still ran and still made lots of money from. Fireweed Brewery was a high-end beer and wine business. Our great-uncle had invested the initial rush of earnings wisely, creating the massive business we now owned.

I gave my head a shake. I didn't need to be contemplating my family. It was part of my identity, and I was the brother who had the least defined role, the one called upon to do the odds and ends jobs. Just a few weeks ago, Blake had called me in a panic because of an equipment failure in the production area. The main brewer was out for the day, so I had shown up and helped him get it fixed. He was pretty hands-on, but I was even more handy than he was.

Blake was leaning hard on our brother Wyatt to come take over as the main brewer. Our current one had plans to move to Juneau with his pregnant wife. We had a smaller location there, and the guy would keep a job with us, but Blake needed someone in Fireweed Harbor. I didn't particularly want that job, but it smarted that he didn't even think to ask me.

Quinn's faith in me was just there. We had slipped so easily into deepening our friendship. It wasn't that we weren't friends growing up. I'd known her, of course. Our families were close, and we'd been friendly. But it wasn't until we had both left town and returned after college that our connection strengthened. I felt like myself with her in a way I didn't with others.

I stepped out of the shower in the small ferry cabin. The ferries were nice in Alaska, but the cabins were utilitarian. The two bunks tucked into the side of the narrow space had just enough room for a small counter with a tiny refrigerator beside it and a microwave. A narrow nook for luggage was across from a tiny bathroom with a sink, a toilet, and a stand-up shower.

I eyed myself in the mirror, running my palm over my cheek as I contemplated whether to shave. Sometimes I grew a trimmed beard during the winter.

I shrugged, deciding against it. It was just a five o'clock shadow. I would shave tomorrow morning before we landed in Whittier for the drive to Willow Brook.

As I dressed, anticipation buzzed through me. Although I very much wanted Quinn, I was doubting how I'd thrown a challenge out to her about deciding what she wanted by tonight.

I never wanted to back down from a dare, and I wanted Quinn with a ferocity that shocked me.

*You've already made it complicated, and you can't undo it.*

I kept telling myself I could handle this. Yet my heart started to want something I'd never contemplated. Even though my two older brothers had defied the odds and fallen in love, I just didn't think it was for me. It was messy and complicated. My self-doubt ran deep. Maybe I couldn't be enough for anyone.

I forcefully kicked those thoughts to the curb and tucked the key to my room in my pocket. A moment later, I stopped by the door immediately beside mine and knocked lightly.

It opened instantly, and Quinn smiled up at me. "Ready?" I asked.

"I opened the door," she replied dryly.

I took a quick breath as she stepped out. Her hair was down, and I wanted to slide my hand into it and kiss her. Right here, right now.

Just then, the door across the hall from her cabin opened. Quinn pulled the door shut on her room, quickly stepping back.

An elderly couple came out and smiled over at us. "Hi," the woman said.

"Hello," Quinn and I said simultaneously. I gestured for the couple to walk ahead of us down the narrow hallway.

A few minutes later, Quinn and I sat at the booth with our dinner trays in the cafeteria as the elderly couple strolled around with their trays. No empty booths were available. I glanced over at Quinn. "We should let them sit with us."

Her gaze followed mine. "Oh, of course."

She scooted to the side of her booth as I did the same, calling over to them, "You're welcome to share our booth."

They sat down, both thanking us profusely. After introductions, we chatted about the weather, the trip, learning that they were from Haines, and taking a trip up to Anchorage to visit family.

"We love taking the ferry," Maria said.

Her husband, Mike, chimed in, "We do!"

"And what about you two?" Maria prompted.

"Oh, we're taking the ferry to Whittier and getting a rental car to go to Willow Brook for a business and family event," I offered.

Maria smiled brightly. "I love seeing young couples. The ferry is good luck for married couples."

I opened my mouth to correct them when Mike nodded in agreement. "We were married on a ferry trip. It's a good luck charm for our whole marriage."

"Oh, that's really sweet," Quinn said. "By the way, we're not married, just friends."

Maria looked back and forth between us. "You're not? Well, you make an excellent couple. I know young people are different, but I can tell by just a few minutes with you two. You're more than friends and make a solid couple."

Once again, Mike chimed in, "Absolutely. My Maria knows when a couple is going to make it." His gaze slid to mine. "Don't let her get away."

I felt Quinn's foot nudge mine under the table and could see the laughter dancing in her eyes. A few minutes later, we had finished our dinners. We said our goodbyes and made our way out of the cafeteria.

"When does the movie start?" Quinn asked a few minutes later as we stood out by the railing. Darkness had fallen, and it was decidedly cold out on the deck. Quinn had wanted to come out and look at the stars.

I glanced at my watch, tapping so that the digital screen was visible. "Ten minutes. We should get in there. It's been a while since I was on the ferry for a movie, but it can fill up pretty quickly."

"We should stop by our rooms and grab a blanket or something."

Quinn leaned her head back and took a deep, audible breath. "I love the air at night on the ferry. It's probably the freshest air in the world."

I took my own breath. The air was crisp and cold, scented with salt from the ocean. The stars shone brightly, and the moon rose in the sky, leaving a glittering path on the ocean's dark surface.

Moments later, we had fetched blankets and pillows from our rooms. Quinn huffed, but let me carry them. We found a spot off to the side toward the back after getting popcorn from the cafeteria.

Quinn smiled over at me when the lights started to dim. "It feels like a slumber party." She adjusted the pillows behind her, leaning against the wall.

The movie started. My mind barely focused on it, with most of my thoughts acutely aware of Quinn's presence beside me under the blanket. My body was tight with anticipation racing in a loop. Need and desire feathered the gas pedal of my body's engine faster and faster.

At some point, Quinn shifted, and her knee brushed against mine. The empty popcorn bucket was by her side. I *had* to touch her. Placing my palm on her thigh, I slid it down to just above her knee. I waited and could feel my heartbeat echoing in a rapid drumroll. She shifted closer, and I glanced down to see her peering at me. Her mouth was right there, just inches away.

# Chapter Eighteen

# QUINN

I could barely breathe and was hot all over with a rushing sound in my ears as my heart pounded. My breath was short and shallow. I felt Kenan's palm on my thigh like a brand. I was wearing a pair of soft, stretchy, swingy pants, sort of like sweatpants but nicer than that. I wanted to be comfortable. I also wanted him to slide his palm down to feel me. My arousal drenched my panties.

I could barely hear the movie in the background with the low voices around us here and there.

"I want to kiss you," he rasped, his lips almost touching mine as he spoke.

"Please," I whispered in return.

"Does that mean what I think it does?"

I knew what he was asking. Were we finally going to take this further? Were we going to see how this played out? My belly swooped, and my heart pounded even faster.

I knew what I wanted. I wanted Kenan. I wanted to see what might happen.

"Yes," I whispered against his lips, just before he brought his mouth fully to mine, claiming it with a deep kiss.

He shifted, angling toward me and sliding his hand into my hair, cupping my nape. He deepened our kiss with his tongue sweeping into my mouth. I arched into him, shifting restlessly, needing more, needing all of it, needing him now. I didn't know how long we kissed until a loud sound in the movie caused us to break apart abruptly. We were both breathing raggedly.

"Let's go," I whispered once I could speak.

We gathered our blankets and pillows and the empty popcorn container. Kenan tossed it in the trash bin on the way out. Seconds later, we practically sprinted down the hallway.

When we reached the doors to our rooms, we stopped and studied each other. My pulse shot into the stratosphere, my heart pounding so hard and fast I could barely think above the cacophony.

A haze of need clouded my thoughts. All I knew was the drumbeat of *Kenan, please, now.* I needed relief from this incessant wanting.

He stared down at me. "Your place or mine?" His voice was raspy, and his lips curled at the corners in a self-deprecating grin.

I snorted. I needed that to relax me, even if it was just barely. "Mine."

"Lead the way."

I was so flustered that I didn't even know where the key was for a moment. I shook my head, rolling my eyes, as I turned away and fumbled in my pockets to find it.

I dropped it on the floor twice before Kenan

leaned down to scoop it up. "Let me try," he said, laughter lacing his words.

I giggled when he dropped the key another time. "Fourth time's a charm," I teased when he fit the key in the lock and opened the narrow door.

"Something like that." He handed me the key, and I set it beside my purse on the small counter just inside the door.

The ferry cabins were small. They were designed for practicality, not for luxury. With Kenan filling the space, it felt even smaller. Topping six feet, he was a tall man with broad shoulders.

I cleared my throat, looking up at him. We both still held pillows and blankets in our arms. Kenan reached for the armful I held. As I let it go, he tossed the pile onto the upper bunk.

I'd stepped out of the way, and my back was against the wall opposite the small bunks. We hadn't made it more than two steps inside, but there was no extra space. Maybe three feet existed between the wall and the two bunk beds built into a tiny alcove.

I took a shaky breath and licked my lips nervously. He turned to face me, his blue eyes darkening as we studied each other. It wasn't as if we didn't already know each other well, but at this moment, it felt as if he swept away all of my defenses with just a flick of his wrist. They felt paper thin and flimsy. That need still drummed through me, chanting his name.

I opened my mouth to say something, anything. In a single stride, he stood right in front of me. He rested one palm on the wall, just above my shoulder.

"Tell me what you're thinking." His low and raspy voice sent a hot shiver chasing over my skin.

I wanted to say something witty as if I wasn't a bundle of nerves twined with a need burning up inside.

As I stared into Kenan's gaze, I found I couldn't laugh my way through this. We knew each other too well. "I'm thinking maybe this is crazy and really stupid, but I want you."

As soon as my words slipped out, anxiety jolted through me. Maybe that was too honest, too direct. I'd exposed myself.

Kenan never looked away from me, lifting his other hand to slide it through the ends of my hair, where it fell over my shoulder.

"Maybe it is crazy, and maybe it is stupid, but I want —"

When he paused, it felt as if cinders drifted down through the air, heating the space around us.

"You," he finished with such deliberate clarity my heart clanged as if in recognition.

He began to dip his head down toward mine before he straightened. His gaze was entirely serious. "If you want to stop at any point, just say so."

My heart tightened. I knew he meant it. I trusted him completely.

I swallowed as I nodded. "The same goes for you," I whispered.

"I'm not going to want to stop," he said flatly.

The quiet stretched just long enough that I thought I might buckle under the pressure of waiting, of wondering, with the need to kiss him rushing through me so fast I could hardly breathe for it.

Finally, *finally*, he shifted closer, erasing the incremental space between us. I arched up to meet him as he lowered his head. His lips brushed over mine once and then again, before he dropped a kiss at one corner of my mouth and then the other.

I felt liquid inside, made of pure need and desire.

After another lingering kiss, he fit his mouth over mine and took command.

His tongue glided against mine, sensually teasing me and blowing past any last barriers left. I got lost in our kiss. He alternated between deep, commanding sweeps of his tongue and dallying with my mouth. He nipped at my bottom lip, dropped lazy kisses on the corners before diving in yet again to take over.

By the time he lifted his head, I was grateful for the wall behind me. Without that and him holding me up, I would've simply melted to the floor.

I took several shaky breaths as we stared at each other. Everything felt suspended, as if it was just us, alone in the whole wide world, caught at this moment. We finally gave in to the living, breathing force of our desire.

We were plastered together, and I could feel the beat of his heart against mine. His eyes fell closed, and he took a deep breath. When they opened again, he brushed my hair back from my cheeks, one hand sliding down my neck to curve over my shoulder.

"I like your shirt," he murmured, a hint of mirth in his voice.

"It's my favorite comfy shirt." I lifted my chin.

I'd worn a fuzzy fleece top with an owl, of all things, on the front. Kenan had actually gotten it for me as a gift. We'd watched *Schitt's Creek*, and I'd nearly peed laughing at the owl shirt that Jocelyn wore for her day at David and Patrick's store.

"I'm a good shopper," he teased.

"I know you are."

"Much as I like it, it's gotta go," he said, his voice turning serious as his eyes darkened.

My belly swooped, and my pulse raced. A moment

later, the owl sweatshirt was on the floor, and we were yanking at each other's clothes. I suppose I should've known it would be like this once we finally gave in. We couldn't get naked fast enough. Maybe later—and it said something that I thought there would be a later— we could savor each other, but not now.

At this moment, it was just a rush to feel *all* of each other.

A few fiery-hot minutes later, Kenan stretched out beside me on the narrow lower bunk. His palm coasted over my belly, the calloused surface sending sparks skittering over my skin. I felt molten. Hot need rushed through me with such intensity, I felt consumed by it.

This was a new feeling for me. I'd never gotten lost in any man's eyes, never gotten lost in the sensation. As much as a part of me found it easier to scoff and dismiss my past encounters as guys who were too rushed and uncaring to elicit such feelings inside me, I also knew I tended to be guarded for whatever reason.

Even though it was slightly terrifying on a level that Kenan kicked those guards away with such ease, I felt it was raw in a way I'd never fathomed. It felt good, so very, *very* good.

"Quinn," Kenan whispered huskily.

I met his eyes, my breath coming in shallow heaves.

"I want you." I felt his words on my lips before he moved on from my mouth, making love to a sweet spot behind my ear that had shivers racing through my body and whimpers coming from my throat.

He teased my breasts, and my nipples literally ached by the time I felt him dropping hot kisses over my belly. One of his palms slid down over my hip and onto my thigh to push my knee to the side.

I trembled, moaning, whimpering, a very needy woman. He kissed the ultra-sensitive skin on the inside of my thigh just before I felt his fingers slide through my folds. I was dripping wet and swollen, and I didn't even care that it was so obvious that he had turned me into a quivering mess of want and desire.

"Oh, Quinn, sweetheart," he whispered against my belly.

Another finger joined the first, sinking into me. My hips rocked into his touch. His mouth was on my sex, and he drove me beyond all reason, all thought. With his fingers skillfully teasing me and his lips and tongue exploring my folds with nothing more than glancing touches over my swollen clit, he reduced me to begging.

"Kenan, please," I gasped.

"Okay, sweetheart," he murmured with a hot kiss just on the inside curve of my hip before he brought his mouth over my sex again. His tongue swirled around my clit before he sucked lightly on it. The pleasure building in wave after wave crested high before breaking and rolling through me. I cried out, my hips bucking sharply, as my climax rocked through my entire body in a burst of fiery release.

I was nearly boneless by the time he rose. He produced a condom and smoothed it on quickly. Even though I'd just had a wildly intense orgasm, I welcomed his weight, wanting the feel of him filling me and to be joined as closely as we could.

Kenan rested on his elbows, brushing my tangled hair back as he looked into my eyes. "Is this still okay?"

"Oh my God, yes!"

I felt him notching at my entrance. My eyes started to fall closed when he said, "I want to see you."

I stared into the rich blue of his gaze as he filled me in one deep surge.

With the echoes of my climax still reverberating in my system, the feel of him inside me was so intense I started to tremble again.

# Chapter Nineteen

# KENAN

Electricity sizzled through me. My attention centered on Quinn's silky, clenching core rippling around me. Her skin was dewy against mine. I stared into her eyes with a sense of intimacy I'd never experienced shimmering around us.

My heart drummed, almost as if it were chanting her name. I held still for a few beats, taking in a quick breath before I drew back and sank into her again. I was already at the very end of my tether, my control about to snap. She gasped, her hips rising to meet mine as I withdrew and filled her once more.

*Fuck me.* The sight of Quinn undone, gasping and whimpering, nearly undid me.

She trembled, crying my name with my next thrust into the very heart of her. My hands laced with her fingers, and her grip tightened with mine. I was already getting familiar with her, and I could feel the quickening inside as I surged into her. I drew back once more for a deep, slow pump, my own release hurtling forward. Lightning sizzled down my spine, tightening my balls.

I released one of her hands, shifting to reach between us. "Kenan!"

"Come for me, sweetheart," I rasped as I teased my fingers over her slippery, swollen clit.

"Oh, oh, oh!"

I gave her just a little more pressure and felt her release as she quivered and trembled all over, her entire body drawing taut just before she cried out and her hips bucked into mine.

With one more thrust into her, I finally let go, my release thundering through me so hard and fast that my mind blanked.

It was all over but for the sound of our ragged breathing and me collapsing against her. I rolled swiftly in the tiny cramped space of her bunk to keep my weight from crushing her. She rested on top of me. It felt as if we'd been cast ashore after a storm with the howl of the wind slowing and the crashing waves quieting. I held her close as my mind slowly adjusted to the moment.

Quinn was warm and soft against me. As the sensations gradually began to ebb, the awareness of what we had just done slammed into me. I had wanted this with Quinn with a fierceness that still startled me. Yet now, I had to face the reality of what *this* meant.

As if Quinn was in tune with me, I felt a barely perceptible tension hum to life in her body. One of my hands sifted through the ends of her hair on her back. It was incremental, just a subtle tightening of the muscles between her shoulder blades. I smoothed my palm down her spine.

She lifted her head, her eyes meeting mine as she curled her palm into a fist and rested it on my chest with her chin atop it. I thought for maybe three whole seconds that the tension would take over the moment.

Everything spun tight before she let out a wondering laugh, and it snapped through the moment.

We laughed together, and I thought maybe we would be okay. "What's so funny?" I asked when she finally stopped laughing.

She took a deep breath, letting it out in a gusty sigh. She lifted one shoulder in a tiny shrug. I could feel every movement because she still rested against me.

"I guess it would've been super awkward if that sucked."

A chuckle rumbled through me again. "Definitely."

Her gaze sobered. "What now?"

I lifted a hand, brushing her hair away from her cheek. "We go to sleep?"

Her cheeks went pink, and she laughed again, burying her face in the curve of my neck. When she lifted her head again, she blinked before nodding.

We disentangled ourselves, and I slipped into the tiny bathroom to dispose of the condom. I was splashing water on my face when I felt her step in behind me. The bathrooms here were very small. The stand-up showers barely had enough room for one person, much less two.

She nudged me with her hip, and I lifted my head as I reached for the towel and dried my face and hands. She followed suit with rinsing her hands and splashing water on her face, looking bashful when her eyes met mine in the mirror a moment later.

"Are you sure you want to go to sleep?" she asked. "Those bunks are tiny. You could sleep up top."

"Not a fucking chance," I murmured as I caught her hand and tugged her out of the bathroom.

It was crowded, but no way was this night ending right now.

# Chapter Twenty

# QUINN

It should've been awkward, super awkward, after all was said and done, and we crossed into best friends having amazing sex. Except it wasn't.

That detail unsettled me even more. Kenan was just easy to be with. I had fallen asleep on his chest and plastered to his side. He propped the pillows so there was a little bit of a bolster behind him on the outside, declaring there was no way he would let me sleep on the outside. "If anyone falls on the floor, it's going to be me."

I cuffed him lightly on the shoulder. "You don't have to be all manly about it and protect me."

He grinned and quipped, "Sure, I do."

He kissed me again. Maybe it would've been easier if we had sex again right then, but we didn't. We fell into a conversation about the winery event. We talked about the couple we met and made bets on what other wildlife we might see on the rest of the ferry trip. He told me we had to plan to go somewhere in Alaska where we could see a polar bear because neither of us had ever seen one.

We'd fallen asleep. I woke up sometime during the night. I wanted to describe what happened in the darkness as sex, but it hadn't felt like that. It felt much deeper. It felt like making love. Our hands explored each other slowly. I'd woken with him wrapped around me from behind. I was already wet with need. When I instinctively nudged my hips toward him and felt his arousal against my bottom, I had to bite my lip from moaning aloud. He nearly teased me to a climax before filling me from behind. I had a sleepy, intense orgasm that rolled through me in deep waves.

The following morning should've felt awkward, but it didn't.

When the ferry docked, we argued over who would drive. Eventually, Kenan said, "Let's flip a coin." He'd waggled his brows.

Another day and hours upon hours later, after the meeting over the land issue, which went smoothly, there was a knock on my door at Wildlands Lodge. Some family members stayed at Archer Cannon's place, but there wasn't much space, so most of us stayed here at the lodge. Situated on the shores of a lake in Willow Brook, the picturesque little town in Southcentral Alaska was just far enough outside of Anchorage that it felt like the edge of the wilderness.

I set my hairbrush down and walked to the door, opening it to find Kenan standing there. His shoulder rested inside the door, and he had one hand tucked in his pocket. My belly flipped and heat blazed through me when his eyes met mine.

"Hey," I said, my voice coming out breathless.

"Hey. Can I come in?"

"Of course." I opened the door wider, and he brushed past me.

As soon as the door clicked shut behind him, he

spun around. I stumbled back instantly, my shoulder blades landing against the door.

He placed both palms on the door beside my shoulders, and his gaze held mine.

"What?" My pulse raced, my breath short and shallow.

"This." He leaned closer until his lips were but a whisper away from mine.

I felt as if electricity sizzled where our lips met. He took my mouth in a lazy, sensual, and utterly devouring kiss. By the time he lifted his head, my knees were weak. I could feel the slick heat of my arousal at the apex of my thighs.

"You can't do that," I whispered a weak, raspy protest.

"I just did," he pointed out.

I rolled my eyes, placing my palm on his chest. I intended to push him back, but the rapid pounding of his heart against my palm arrested my movement for a few seconds. Maybe it didn't make sense, but I was relieved that his pulse felt as wildly out of control as mine did.

I pressed just enough that he stepped back. I ducked under his arm and stepped around him. I walked to the windows of my hotel room, curling my arms around my waist as I looked out. The view here was beautiful. Willow Brook, like so much of Alaska, had mountains nearby. With winter on the way, snow already blanketed the peaks.

The lake was frozen. The sunset reflected on the ice, a blurry shimmer of lavender and deep pink.

"We have to talk," I said when I felt him stop beside me.

"I thought you might say that."

I glanced up at him and looked away again. "I'm

not ready for us to be public. If everything goes to shit for us, I'd rather people not know."

I was nervous, uncomfortably so, and my arms tightened around my waist.

"Do you really think it'll go to shit?" he asked.

Even though it was difficult, I forced myself to face him. "Kenan, you're my best friend. I know we've already crossed those boundaries, but you've never had a serious relationship, for a very good reason, at least, according to you," I pointed out.

"Neither have you," he returned.

I knew him well enough to know he was feeling defensive. I could hear it in his voice. "I know I haven't," I said quietly. "But it's not like I have my pick of men the way you have your pick of women. If you wanted to get married, you could probably get married tomorrow. Plenty of women would line up to sign up for that. It's not that easy for me."

A muscle ticked in his jaw as he swallowed. "It's not that easy for me. You're beautiful. I just don't think you see that."

I took a quick breath. "Whatever. We could debate this. That's not all that's at stake. I work for your family, and I like my job. I don't want things to get awkward there. I'd rather not have this be common knowledge. Not now."

Kenan finally nodded. "I understand. We're already best friends, so we can just keep it that way publicly. We see each other all the time."

"No PDA," I said firmly.

Kenan's lips quirked at the corners. "Fine. Understood. Shall we go?"

"Yes."

# Chapter Twenty-One

# KENAN

Just as Quinn reached for the door, I caught her by the elbow. She glanced up at me. "What is it?"

"Just a sec."

I palmed her cheek before bending low to capture her mouth with a kiss. I'd meant for this to be controlled, just a tease. I should've known better. The moment our lips met, I was gone. Her tongue darted out to tease mine. It was a damn good thing I could put my other hand against the door behind her because that was about the only thing that kept me standing.

By the time we broke apart, we were both heaving. "What the hell?" she mused between gulps of air.

"You said no PDA," I managed to retort as I dragged in another breath. "I had to get a little dose before we left."

She burst out laughing. "Oh my God, is this how it's going to be?"

I chuckled as we both straightened and stepped apart. "Yes."

"Is that a promise?" she teased, the glint in her eyes making me want to kiss her all over again.

As it was, I had to get my raging hard-on under control. "Absolutely."

It was supposed to be a joke, and it was. But as we stared at each other, that unsettling intimacy shimmied to life in the air between us.

I cleared my throat. "We should go."

I held the door for her, my hand reflexively reaching to touch her, to slide down over the sweet curve of her bottom and coax her forward.

———

"Well, we pulled it off," Adam said from my side.

Glancing at him, I grinned. "Archer and Chase pulled it off," I pointed out.

Adam chuckled. "They're family, so that counts as we. You and Quinn helped negotiate the contract for this building, and I ran the numbers," he added.

"Fair enough." I let my gaze arc about the space. It looked good, really good.

Fireweed Industries had purchased a defunct storage garage on the outskirts of town. We'd needed something big enough to eventually open a small production area here.

It would be a much smaller production and distribution warehouse than the one in Fireweed Harbor. We wanted them to be able to produce small batches of beer for sale right here in the brewery and winery, in addition to local distribution in Anchorage.

Archer and Chase had headed up the renovation. The restaurant and bar looked nice. The space had an industrial vibe. They'd polished all of the visible exposed beams and venting and added additional windows that offered a view of the mountains and a glacial lake nearby.

The space was decorated with fabric arts mounted on the walls and furnished with round wooden tables and a wide polished wooden bar that ran the length of the back of the space with an additional one in the center. The opening event was crowded. The locals had filled the space within minutes of opening.

Archer stopped beside us, lifting a bottle of beer in a mock toast. "We're busy," he said lightly.

I grinned. "Seriously. You and Chase pulled off a great opening."

Archer's wife, Phoebe, appeared, hearing the tail end of my comment. She leaned up to press a kiss on Archer's cheek, the love and pride shining in her gaze. "That's what I told him. This was a lot of work, and you did an incredible job."

"We had a lot of help from David," Archer replied. He gestured toward David, the longtime chef for the winery restaurant in Fireweed Harbor who had shifted into an administrative role within the past year or so. He was talking with some staff behind the bar. "David organized most of this, while Chase and I handled the local logistics and staffing. Blake was a huge help as well."

"He'll be your main point of contact for getting the production up and running here," Adam commented.

"I'm going to let Chase lead that," Archer said just as Chase, our half brother, appeared beside us.

Our father had a summer fling with Chase's mother before he met our mother, but none of us knew about him until McKenna did a genealogy test for fun.

"Chase is leading what?" Chase prompted with a grin.

"Production," Archer replied.

"Oh yeah. I'm actually looking forward to that. As it is, I've just been doing whatever is needed around here."

"I told him he's been like you for us here," Archer said, nudging his chin toward me. "The everything guy, like an everything bagel."

"Oh, I love everything bagels," Phoebe enthused. "They are the best."

We collectively chuckled. Just then, Quinn appeared in my line of sight. She weaved her way through the crowd, stopping to say something to Blake and Fiona by the bar in the center. Every cell in my body fired up when my eyes landed on her. My entire system felt like engines revving at the start of a race.

I recalled her comments before we left about no PDA and how she wanted us to be a secret. It wasn't that I didn't understand. I did. But it chafed. More so because I understood her hesitation about me.

Adam said something beside me, dragging my attention away from Quinn. Being my twin, we had a closeness that I didn't really share with anyone else. When you were a twin, a bond, a closeness just happened. Twins ran in our mother's side of the family. Our family tree had several sets in the generations above us.

I wasn't even present when Adam broke his arm playing baseball in middle school, so I didn't know exactly what happened. It wasn't quite like that. Yet that day, I had told a mutual friend in school that I thought something happened to Adam.

I avoided sharing the deep cynicism I felt about love with anyone in my family. We all carried collective survivor's guilt about what happened to Jake. As much as I loved my siblings and believed that family was important, my way of coping was becoming the one who fixed everything. I was the fix-it guy, the guy who smoothed everything over. I didn't have enough faith in myself to have kids. I carried a deep worry that, somehow, I just couldn't be everything for everyone, certainly not for someone I loved.

Quinn knew that about me, and I knew her understanding of my fears was the reason she had her doubts. I couldn't imagine life without her now. I still couldn't believe what I'd proposed, that we see what happened. Now, I wanted it *all* with her. Yet that deep-seated fear that I couldn't be enough made me fear that I truly couldn't, that I would be the one who would make it all fall apart. While Quinn worried about what other people might think if things didn't work for us, I worried that I would feel like I had not been enough for her, that I might fail her.

I forced my attention to the conversation around me, just as a few of Chase and Phoebe's friends from their days as hotshot firefighters appeared. They both still filled in on the crews in a pinch. Conversation carried on, and I managed to fall into the easy rhythm of casual talk.

A few minutes later, Quinn appeared, standing beside Wyatt. It was good to see Wyatt, always. He glanced down at her, giving her a friendly smile. "Well, hey Quinn, smartest woman in the room," he said with a wink.

"Why do you always say that?" she asked in return.

"Because I'm pretty sure it's true," he said.

"You don't really know that, though," she pointed out

Wyatt's brows hitched up as he cocked his head to the side. "I'm pretty sure I do."

Quinn rolled her eyes. "So how's life as a hotshot

firefighter?" she asked, dividing her gaze between Wyatt and Griffin, who was standing beside him.

They shrugged simultaneously. Like me and Adam, they weren't identical. Griffin shared the same gray eyes and dark blond hair coloring as the rest of our siblings, while Wyatt had dark hair and blue eyes like our mother and me.

McKenna appeared, stepping between Wyatt and Griffin. She looped her arms through theirs, squeezing as she beamed from one to the other. "You guys need to come home."

Griffin chuckled. "We will." Wyatt finished Griffin's sentence with, "When the time is right."

Blake meandered over with Fiona, chiming in with, "I need you guys at the winery and brewery."

"Whatever for?" Quinn prompted.

For fuck's sake, her voice alone sent a sizzle of heat through me. It wasn't as if the sound of Quinn's voice was new to me. Yet I was acutely aware of its throaty quality and the subtle rasp.

I distantly heard Blake explaining that our main brewer was moving to Juneau with his wife because she was expecting a baby and they wanted to be closer to family.

I felt an elbow nudge my side and glanced over at Adam. "What?"

"You're staring."

"What?" I repeated, not even catching on that he was teasing me.

"At Quinn. You know, the friend you swore you'd never be interested in."

I scuffed my toe on the floor and quickly glanced out the windows. Of course, Adam would notice. He already knew I'd kissed her.

As if he could read my mind—which sometimes I

wondered if he could, and I was pretty sure he wondered the same of me at times—he added, "I'm not the only one who's noticed. It's obvious."

"Shut up," I muttered.

Just then, a server walked by with a tray of beers. When he paused beside our group, I snagged one and took a long swallow. By some lucky miracle, as far as I knew, no one else in our family was prone to overdrinking like Jake.

Blessedly, Adam dropped any further comments about Quinn. There were enough people around to keep me distracted. I was uncomfortably aware of the effort it took not to keep glancing at Quinn and not to let my gaze linger on her.

Eventually, the event wound down, and we all filtered away. Some in the group made plans to meet in the bar at Wildlands Lodge where we were staying. I made the excuse that I was tired. As I walked through the reception area at the lodge to take the stairs up to my room, Wyatt fell into step beside me. I glanced over. "It's good to see you."

He flashed a smile. "Ditto."

"Mom would love it if you guys came home," I said.

His smile stretched a little wider. "We know. I'm seriously considering taking Blake up on coming back to do the brewing."

"You could do that, and Griffin could handle the wine," I replied. "The guy he has now does both, but he's stretched pretty thin." We had paused at the base of the stairs and began walking up together.

"He mentioned that," Wyatt replied. "Maybe next spring. We have to make a decision if we're going to stay on before fire season kicks in next year."

"I vote for you to come home." I paused on the landing of the second floor. "But I also understand you love what you're doing. Enjoy it while you can. It's not a career you can do forever anyway."

Wyatt chuckled. "Definitely not." He slipped his key card out of his front pocket, spinning it between his fingers. "I'm on this floor." He paused, studying me for a few beats. "By the way, it's obvious you and Quinn might be taking things to the next level."

I didn't even notice my mouth had dropped open until he reached over with the key card and tapped the bottom of my chin. I snapped it shut and rolled my eyes. "What are you talking about?" I hedged.

"Dude, you stared at her every chance you had. You've been besties for years now. Don't screw it up. I always thought you'd make a good couple anyway."

With that, Wyatt winked and turned, calling over his shoulder, "Good night."

I jogged up the stairs to the top floor. As I turned down the hallway, my pulse picked up its pace. I had been so studiously avoiding Quinn, that I didn't know if she was in the bar or if she was in her room.

My room was beside hers. I couldn't help but wonder if McKenna had been aware of that. Not that McKenna made our reservations, but she would've been the one to give any instructions to Tish.

The stretch of hallway in front of our rooms was empty. Disappointment sliced through me. Aside from trying to keep up appearances, tonight's effort at avoiding Quinn meant I'd missed just hanging out with her. Because she was my best friend, if I'd been behaving normally, we would've chatted most of the night.

I let myself into my room, kicking off my shoes and shrugging out of my jacket. Before turning on the light, I crossed over to the windows. It was dark out now with the half-moon casting a glow on the snowy peaks of a mountain range in the distance. Turning away, I flicked on the lights and lifted my phone, tapping out a quick text to Quinn.

**Me:** *I need to see you.*

If I'd spoken aloud, the words would've been terse, taut from the need bound up tightly inside me.

I tossed my phone on the dresser across from the foot of the bed and tried to take a slow breath, anything to quell the impatience and restless need kicking up a storm inside me.

The second my phone vibrated on the dresser, I spun around to snatch it.

**Quinn:** *Should I do Morse code on the wall between our rooms?*

I smiled, a piercing sense of joy rising inside.

**Me:** *I'll be right there. Let me in when I knock.*

I grabbed my key card, not even bothering to put my shoes on as I slipped out of my room and immediately knocked on Quinn's door. My phone vibrated with her reply as she opened it.

**Quinn:** *Just get over here!*

I was in her room in a flash, kicking the door shut behind me and cupping her cheeks as I dipped my head to claim her mouth in a kiss.

# Chapter Twenty-Two

# QUINN

I moaned into Kenan's mouth, frantically arching up, trying to get as close to him as I possibly could. Our kiss was messy, overwhelming, and deep. Our tongues tangled and our teeth clanked together before we finally broke apart.

Kenan still cupped my cheeks as he stared into my eyes.

"Oh my God!" I gasped.

He said, "I missed you tonight."

I knew what he meant. If we hadn't been trying so hard to avoid each other tonight, we would've mostly been together as we chatted with our mutual friends and his family. Instead, we'd avoided each other. In his case, I knew it was because I ordered him not to give me any affection. I'd never been so into a man that I stared at him from across a room. It was as if Kenan was a magnet and I was the opposing force drawn to him.

Over and over and over again, my eyes had been drawn to him, and I'd had to tear them away. Adam had caught us. I'd seen him look from me to Kenan and back again before he winked at me and nudged Kenan hard with his elbow.

I knew without a word being spoken that Adam sensed what was going on for us. I didn't mind him knowing. Although we didn't have the same kind of friendship I had with Kenan, I trusted Adam and knew he wouldn't gossip.

Lifting a palm, I trailed my fingers in a soothing caress over the stubbled line of Kenan's jaw and down over the side of his neck, where it came to rest just between his collarbones. I could feel the thrum of his pulse racing under my fingertips.

"I know," I whispered. "I missed you too."

My belly felt funny, and my heart flipped over in my chest. It felt as if we were racing into this, holding hands and stumbling down a hill where we couldn't catch our balance. We already knew each other so well, yet this was also intensely new and unfamiliar. I felt vulnerable and deeply exposed.

I took a shaky breath, trying to tell myself I needed to step back, but I couldn't. As frightening as this was in some ways, I felt completely safe and protected with Kenan. I knew he would take care of me and never hurt me. Yet he could decimate me because of how I felt.

Our gazes remained locked as his forehead fell to mine, and he whispered something against my lips.

I needed to take control of this somehow. I slid my palm down his chest and over the muscled planes of his abdomen to stroke over the hard ridge of his arousal. I deftly opened his jeans, sliding the zipper down and slipping my hand inside his boxers. I savored the way his cock leaped under my touch and the feel of his skin, velvety soft and hot.

I nudged him back with my knee. We were barely inside my room, and the door was right behind him.

Kenan's eyes were on mine as I knelt in front of him, shoving his jeans and boxers down, just enough for his cock to spring free. A bead of cum glistened on his tip, and I leaned forward to swipe it with my tongue. I savored the control and power I felt racing through me when he let out a ragged groan and his head thumped against the door.

I dragged my tongue along the underside of his cock before swirling around the tip and sucking lightly on the thick crown. We still gazed at each other, and I angled my head to the side as I licked from the base of his cock to the tip. I could taste the salty tang when a drop of cum danced over my tongue. His fingers slid into my hair. I loved the subtle sting on my scalp from his grip. Every sensation brought me deeper into my body, deeper into the storm that Kenan stirred up inside.

He growled my name when I sucked him deep inside my mouth. I curled my fist at the base as I settled in to suck and tease him. He gasped my name again, his fingers tightening in my hair. One of his palms slapped against the door, and his hips thrust toward me, his release spurting into my mouth. A moment later, I drew back, releasing him with a pop.

We stared at each other. His breath came in heaves, and I was acutely aware of how wet I was. My panties were soaked, and I needed him inside me. Now.

I stumbled away from the door to the bed. I tossed my shirt to the floor, and he yanked on my jeans, murmuring, "I need to be inside you."

My jeans were only half around my hips, as I heard him yanking his wallet out and tossing it to the floor.

A second later, he rolled on a condom. He bent me over on the bed. I had one knee resting on it. There was a tight friction from where my jeans were still half around my knees.

"Oh, sweetheart," he groaned when he teased his fingers in my folds.

I rocked my hips back, crying out. I was already so close to coming; my release was right there. He pumped twice with his fingers before withdrawing his touch. I cried out, bereft.

"Kenan, hurry," I begged, not even recognizing the woman I was when I was in thrall with him, so tied up with desire that I forgot everything but him.

"Right here, sweetheart."

I felt the thick press of his crown at my entrance followed by the slow slide of him filling me. I threw my head back as I cried out and pressed back into him. His palm slid up my back, his fingers tangling into my hair as he seated himself more deeply.

Everything was a rush as he began to thrust into me. He reached around, teasing his fingers over my clit. My release came in a noisy burst. I heard myself crying his name. He thrust once more to fill me as we shuddered, and he curled around me.

We collapsed on the bed together, with Kenan still inside me. We lay there, gasping for breath.

"Is it always going to be like this?" I asked a few minutes later when I could finally catch my breath.

He smoothed my hair away from my cheek, his lips landing on the back of my neck, just behind my ear, as he murmured, "I don't know."

We disentangled ourselves and actually finished undressing before he tugged me into the shower. He kissed me lazily under the water running down around us, and then we tumbled into bed, falling asleep wrapped up together.

When I woke in the darkness, he was curled up behind me, holding me in his embrace. I felt safer and more secure than I'd ever felt in my life. I wanted to sleep like this every night, with my very best friend.

A sense of trepidation slipped through me. Because maybe this felt good for me, but what if it didn't last?

# Chapter Twenty-Three

# QUINN

I caught myself tracing my fingertip along the surface of my bracelet. I told myself I was just polishing it. Ha! I was nervous, really nervous. A moment later, a light knock sounded on the door to the small examination room where I waited at the doctor's office.

"Come in!" I called.

A woman stepped in, her smile warm as she glanced over. She wore the requisite white lab coat, with her name, Nelly Thomas, MD, stitched onto it in blocky script. She held a computer tablet in her hand and sat across from me at a wheeled stand with a computer monitor mounted to the side. She promptly swung it in front of her and set the tablet on the counter behind her.

"I'm Dr. Thomas. You were referred over by your OB/GYN in Fireweed Harbor, correct?" she asked.

I nodded, lacing my hands together as I glanced down. My legs were crossed with one of my feet bobbing in the air. I quickly uncrossed them and planted both feet firmly on the floor as if I could will my anxiety away. I cleared my throat.

"I get a lot of referrals from her. She could actually do my job."

"Oh, I can work with her if that's better."

Dr. Thomas smiled over at me before her eyes dipped down to the computer screen. She tapped a few keys on the keyboard. "She could, but she tells me she prefers to do the generalist practice. So here's my spiel about IVF..." she began.

Approximately half an hour later, I had the details of the process. I was considered a prime candidate—healthy and fairly young, and the initial tests showed I didn't have any issues with my ovulation. To start, she set me up with some medication to prime my fertility and sent me away with a link to review my options for sperm donors.

I couldn't believe it. I was going to do this. Every time I had started to think about Kenan on the short flight from Fireweed Harbor to Juneau today, I batted those thoughts away. He had told me time and again that he didn't want kids. He loved all of his siblings and said he would be an excellent uncle to the passel of kids his siblings would produce. I didn't know what would happen with us, but I wanted a baby, and I wanted to be a mother.

The timing of what was happening between Kenan and me muddled the issues around motherhood for me. Maybe we would get this out of our systems and realize we were meant to be friends and hopefully not obliterate our friendship. Or things might feel better, but we would discover we couldn't work out because I wanted to have kids, and he didn't.

I tried to ignore the doubts dancing along the edges of my thoughts time and again. Normally, I would've had a conversation with Kenan about this.

Yet this one thing felt too personal, even before this pesky chemistry had flared up between us.

I took a breath as I waited to check out at the reception area at this busy office in Juneau. This fertility doctor was busy. A part of me felt like I was giving up on something by doing this now, but I didn't want to contemplate that.

I took care of my payment and left the office, slinging my purse over my shoulder as I stepped onto the sidewalk in Juneau. The downtown area here was cute, with colorful signs and shops.

I had a good excuse for being here. We had a meeting with one of our smaller distributors in Juneau to sign an updated contract. Blake was also down here for this, checking in as usual.

I walked down the sidewalk and was startled when I heard my name. Glancing up, I saw Kenan and Blake approaching. I masked my surprise and tried to quell the jolt of fiery recognition that sizzled to life inside me.

"Hi!" I stopped in front of them. "I didn't know you were coming," I said to Kenan, trying to keep my voice casual.

"Blake wanted some company. We're touring a new building for the expansion since our brewer from Fireweed Harbor is moving here."

"I didn't know you were thinking about that." I shifted my attention to Blake.

"I just thought of it this morning. I heard from the distributor that one of the breweries here is closing up shop, so I thought I'd check out the location."

"Did you have another appointment?" Kenan asked.

I glanced over my shoulder, biting back a sigh.

"Oh, nothing much, just an annual appointment." I shrugged.

My answer had to be good enough. I hoped. Kenan had always been nosy, so I hoped he took my answer at face value and left it alone.

I glanced at my watch. "Well, we have an hour. Have you guys had lunch?"

"Nope," Blake replied. "We just came out from the location and saw you, so we crossed the street to meet you. Should we grab lunch together?"

"Sure. There's that soup and sandwich place right down the street." We fell into step together and began walking. "What flight did you guys take down this morning?"

The frequency of flights out of so many smaller communities was unique to Alaska. Although Fireweed Harbor had a population of roughly four thousand, flights came in and out of town to Juneau and several other smaller communities in Southeast Alaska every other hour. That wasn't unusual at all.

I remembered traveling with my father to the Bethel area of Alaska. By any stretch, it was a very rural area. Over one-hundred flights bounced in and out of that tiny town daily, fanning out to the array of Alaskan Native villages in the area.

A few minutes later, we were seated at a small table in the café. It was small enough that I could feel the heat of Kenan's presence beside me. I wished I could order my hormones to behave, but they weren't listening to reason.

I'd foolishly thought maybe giving in to this crazy conflagration of chemistry burning between us would help tamp it down, as if it would burn up quickly to ashes. Instead, it seemed only to have fed the fire. My body knew what it felt like to give in. It felt very, very good.

I silently groaned. I hated my constant worry that people would notice. I tried to tell myself our friendship would mask it.

After we had ordered, Blake was talking about something. I honestly wasn't paying attention. "Quinn?" he prompted.

"Yes?" I whipped my gaze to his.

"I was just asking if everything was all lined up for the contract," he clarified.

"Oh, of course. They sent over the final one. We could've signed it electronically, but you know how I like to look at the final version."

"I know," Blake replied. "For local stuff, I prefer to do the in-person thing. I feel so disconnected otherwise."

"Agreed. As long as the weather's good, I don't mind traveling. I'll be back in the office in Fireweed Harbor within the hour after our meeting."

Kenan's knee bumped mine, and it felt like a jolt of lightning sizzling up my thigh. The server stopped by the table to deliver our drinks, and I slid my gaze to Kenan's, narrowing my eyes because I was confident he had done that on purpose. He winked before sliding his palm onto my thigh.

I nudged him hard with my knee in return. I should've known better. He moved his palm farther up my thigh. I was wearing a pair of jeans tucked into boots, nothing risqué. I ignored him. I forced the conversation onto a particularly dry human resources issue because we were in the midst of updating policies at the corporation.

Unfortunately, Kenan kept his palm on my thigh. His touch felt like a brand with heat suffusing me. I refused to nudge him again with my knee because I knew that would only reinforce the distraction.

At one point, I saw Blake's eyes flick from Kenan to me curiously, and I prayed he wasn't picking up on anything.

# Chapter Twenty-Four

# KENAN

A few hours later, Blake, Quinn, and I were back in Fireweed Harbor. We had flown back on the plane together. Quinn had hopped in her car, making some excuse about needing to get back to the office for a scheduled phone conference.

We were driving back when Blake commented, "So what the hell is going on with you and Quinn?"

I kept my gaze trained out the passenger window where I was already watching the landscape roll by. "What do you mean?"

"Don't make it so easy on me," he chided. "You've been close friends for years, but something is different."

My jaw clenched, and I took a breath, willing the tension to ease. "We're just friends," I insisted.

Blake turned onto the side street that led to the parking area behind the main offices for Fireweed Industries. A moment later, he turned off the SUV. When he didn't make a move to get out, I glanced over.

"What?" I was irritated.

His gaze was understanding as he studied me. "I'm sure if something has happened that you both want to keep it quiet. Obviously, I understand. But don't hurt Quinn."

I let out an annoyed breath. "I would never hurt her," I said sharply.

"I'm sure you wouldn't mean to. But you and Quinn are different. Everything is always casual for you."

"Hey, that's how you used to be," I pointed out.

"Yep, and then I fell in love with Fiona. I'm just saying that Quinn is a big part of your life as a friend, and she works for us. It could get really messy if things get weird."

"It's not like I don't know that." I shifted my shoulders, trying to ease the tension bundling at the base of my neck and between my shoulder blades. "You know how much she means to me." My heart twisted in my chest.

"I know that," Blake said, his tone completely serious. He shook his head slowly, letting out a disbelieving chuckle. "I can't believe this, but I think I need to worry about you more than her."

"What the hell do you mean by that?"

"I'm not going to pressure you to tell me what's happened, if anything, but I get the sense you're falling for her, and you never expected this to happen. I know you didn't because you've always sworn you were just friends and there would never be more." He reached over, clapping me on the shoulder and squeezing firmly. "If you need any advice on romance, I'm here for you."

"Oh my fucking God," I muttered under my breath. "Can we end this conversation now?"

Blake chuckled as he climbed out of his SUV. With

a wave, he headed over to the brewery and I walked into the main offices, intending to scout out Quinn. I knew she'd been deliberately vague about her doctor's appointment. I'd seen the sign on the doctor's office when she walked out. I'd already looked it up.

Minutes later, I knocked lightly on Quinn's office door. I could see through the windows flanking her door that she was, in fact, on a phone call. Her eyes lifted from her computer screen, and she gestured for me to come in.

As I was closing the door behind me, I heard her saying, "Thank you, I'll give you a call if we have any additional questions."

She tapped the button on her phone to end the call, lifting the receiver and setting it down again, a habit she had to ensure she didn't accidentally leave a call line open.

"And here I thought you were bullshitting," I said as I crossed the office and stopped in front of her desk. My lips curled into a smile automatically. I was in a room with Quinn, and that alone elicited a smile.

"Bullshitting about what?" Quinn leaned back in her chair as she gestured to the one I stood beside. "You know you can sit down."

"I was waiting for you to offer," I teased.

She rolled her eyes. "To my point."

When she looked at me with her lips pursed just a little bit and her eyes narrowed behind her glasses, a look I knew well, a jolt of lust bolted through me. Fuck me. I'd thought and re-thought about what was happening between us. The way my body reacted to her was still startling. I'd honestly believed that the edge of this need would start to wear off. If anything, my need for her was getting sharper with each encounter between us serving to hone its blade.

"I thought you were bullshitting about your call." I waited just long enough that her brows arched up.

She picked up this little wand she kept on her desk. She tipped it up and watched as the glitter fell inside the narrow tube. "Why would I bullshit about that?" She held my gaze.

I took a quick breath. "I don't know. Why were you at an OB/GYN office in Juneau? Isn't your doctor here in Fireweed Harbor?"

Her eyes dropped from mine, and she started spinning that little wand in her fingers. The nervous motion was a dead giveaway that she was hiding something. "Like I told you, it was an annual appointment."

Her eyes lifted to mine again. I wanted to push, to demand that she explain, but I sensed she wasn't going to tell me anything. Although we were close friends, I wasn't prone to quizzing her about medical appointments. I sensed she was keeping something from me and that bothered me. A lot.

I shrugged. "Fine. Just curious."

"Just curious, huh?"

Now, I felt like the one being questioned. I waggled my brows. "Well, yeah. We haven't had the birth-control conversation. Maybe we could discuss options."

Her eyes lifted to mine, narrowing. "Maybe we'll stick with condoms."

I bit the inside of one cheek as I studied her. "Fine. I mean —" I began again.

"Kenan, this is all new territory for us. Don't blow it by getting pushy about that right now."

I felt legitimately chastised, even though I didn't care if we used condoms forever. I was just trying to find a way to get more information. "Understood. I reserve the right to find out what the hell you're hiding from me later."

Quinn lifted her chin. It felt as if she was daring me.

I waited. She finally rolled her eyes and set the wand on her desk.

"My medical information is my business," she said primly.

# Chapter Twenty-Five

# QUINN

Every time I contemplated that conversation with Kenan in my office, I felt uncomfortable. Because I *was* hiding something. I wanted a baby, and I knew he didn't. I didn't have faith that we were going to work out as it was, which made it all the crazier and ridiculous that I'd let things go to the next level with him.

Yet when I tried to talk myself back out of that, I didn't want to. It felt good, so very good.

I wondered if I'd always had a hidden thing for him that I'd buried deep inside. When it finally broke through, it just wouldn't be denied. I would probably never know that.

The following afternoon, I stopped by the pharmacy to pick up the medication intended to optimize my fertility. I felt like I was engaging in a top-secret mission.

"I've stopped by this pharmacy maybe hundreds of times," I muttered to myself in my car.

It was, in fact, where I usually picked up my birth control pills. Aside from it being a pharmacy, it was also a general convenience store. It was open an hour later than the regular grocery store. Many people stopped by here for small things they needed.

I wouldn't even be thinking about this if it weren't for Kenan and him sensing I was keeping something from him. I'd told him my medical information was my business, which was true, but my conscience kept pricking at me.

I shook away my worries and strolled into that pharmacy with my chin lifted and a confident stride. It was no big deal for me to be here. I walked to the back, where the pharmacy was, and got in line.

The young woman checking me out gave me a curious look. Or perhaps that was my own paranoia. I assured myself it didn't matter, even if she was curious.

As I was walking out, I glanced over and saw Kenan walking down the sidewalk. He appeared to be just coming out of Spill the Beans Café. Fuckity fuck.

My car was still parked behind Fireweed Industries, which was behind me. I kept walking as if I were going to Spill the Beans Café. I didn't need him wondering if I stopped by the pharmacy.

As he approached, my eyes tracked him. He was one of those guys who always looked at ease in his body. I'd never really thought much about Kenan's appearance, or so I'd convinced myself. My eyes lingered on his shoulders. I knew the way his muscles felt flexing underneath my palms. I forcefully kicked those thoughts to the curb, as heat instantly suffused my entire body.

He stopped in front of me when we met on the sidewalk. "Hey, Quinn."

There was a teasing glint in his eyes, and butterflies tickled my belly. "Hey, Kenan," I replied as I looked up at him.

I wanted to kiss him. Right this very second. I

didn't want to hide this. I had to instantly shackle that urge. I was the one who demanded we keep this private. It needed to stay that way because the end was a foregone conclusion.

"Where are you headed?" he asked.

I pointed over his shoulder. "Spill the Beans."

"You could spill the beans," he quipped with an exaggerated brow waggle.

I rolled my eyes. "There are no beans to spill, but I do need some coffee. Is that where you just were?"

He shook his head. "Nope. I was at the post office. I was going into the café, but I saw you and figured we could go together."

"Fine," I said too sharply.

He turned, falling into step beside me. "Fine? I think that means you don't want to have coffee with me."

"Of course, I want to have coffee with you. We would normally get coffee together a few times a week," I pointed out as I glanced sideways at him.

"True, but I thought we were keeping things on the down low."

"We're keeping PDA on the down low. It'll be weird if we act like we wouldn't normally act," I ground out.

He nudged me with his elbow. "Very true."

Kenan held the door for me when we got to the front of the café. His hand lightly rested on my back as I passed by, coaxing me forward with a subtle touch. I was sure he had touched me that way before, but just now, the touch felt intimate.

A few minutes later, we had ordered. Haven was having coffee with Rhys at a table in the corner. She waved us over, just as Rosie came in.

Between my anxiety about my lying by omission

with Kenan about my IVF plans and the furtive quality of our sneaking around, I was a bundle of nerves. Rhys and Kenan chatted about something related to work. I busied myself nibbling on a scone and sipping my coffee. At one point, Haven caught my eye. She smiled at me, but I sensed she was distracted.

Kenan's palm was still resting on my thigh, and I shifted restlessly. I didn't think he was paying attention, but he moved his hand back and forth in a soothing caress. My heart twisted in my chest. I already cared way too much about Kenan. If anyone had asked me before this whole thing started with us, I would've said I loved him like a friend. He was one of the most important people in my life, the person I thought to call first about anything big or small.

Now, that sense of love was deepening and tangling within the intimacy and passion I felt with him. I took a quick swallow of coffee. The cheery bell jingled above the door, and I reflexively glanced over to see McKenna coming in. She waved over at us as her gaze arced about the space. *Great, just freaking great, one more person.*

With everyone we encountered, I worried about who might catch onto what had changed between Kenan and me. Only moments later, McKenna stood beside our table. It just so happened she stopped beside me. I felt her gaze dip down and land on Kenan's palm resting on my thigh. Heat flashed into my cheeks, and I refused to look up at her, studying my coffee. I wanted to knock his hand away, but that would only draw more attention.

"Have you shown them?" McKenna asked Haven.

"Shown us what?" Kenan prompted.

Haven grinned as she slipped her phone out of her

purse and tapped the screen to open it. She handed her phone to Rhys first.

"Why does he get to see first?" Kenan teased.

Rhys glanced over. "Because."

McKenna chuckled. "Because they're in love." She looked around the café before her eyes came back to mine. "It's the new design. We're redoing all the signage for Fireweed Industries, including the winery."

"Is that the surprise?" Rhys asked as he looked at Haven.

She waggled her brows. "Absolutely, but I didn't want to show you until McKenna and I settled on something. What do you think?"

"I love it," Rhys said as he handed her phone back to her.

"Of course you love it. You're whipped," Kenan grumbled from my side.

"Let me see." I shifted, deftly knocking Kenan's palm off my knee with one hand as I reached across the table with the other.

I glanced at the screen as Haven handed her phone to me. "Oh, this is perfect!" I exclaimed.

"This is just for the main business," she said.

"What are you doing for the winery?"

"Just swipe for the next photo. No matter which direction you go, all of the photos in there are for this design."

Haven had used a bold font for the main corporate design with a fireweed twined through the corner on one side. The winery and brewery had a more whimsical font.

I studied them before glancing back at her. "I love these!"

I glanced at Kenan as he was peering over my

shoulder. "These are fantastic," he enthused, smiling over at Haven.

Her cheeks were pink as she smiled. "Thank you. On the one hand, it's just words, so it may seem like it should be quick and easy, but trying to find a balance between business and capturing the feel of the place is what I was after."

Behind the lettering for the main corporate sign were jagged peaks, the skyline of Fireweed Harbor. "You absolutely succeeded," I said as I passed her phone back over.

Kenan's palm slid back onto my thigh, and he squeezed lightly. I steeled myself to handle the need rioting inside me. Conversation carried on around us. Meanwhile, between my anxiety and the arousal that just wouldn't quit whenever I happened to be near Kenan, I was beyond flustered.

"Speaking of image, we need somebody to get the Christmas decorations up on the main building. I saw the winery is ready for the holidays, but we're behind the ball on the offices," McKenna commented.

I had never in my life worried about Christmas decorations, but I needed something to talk about. "We do need to take care of that."

I could feel the heat of Kenan's gaze on me, and knowing I needed to make things seem normal with us, I glanced up. "What?"

"I didn't know you worried all that much about Christmas decorations," he said.

I gestured around the café. They had lights strung in the windows and a crab pot fashioned into a Christmas tree glittering on one of the porch tables. Lights decorated the trees outside as well. "When the snow falls soon, it looks pretty. I'm just saying."

He squeezed my thigh lightly, and heat pooled in

my belly. Somehow, I didn't even know how, I got through the social interaction. It felt like walking a tightrope. When the group broke apart, Kenan went to use the restroom on our way out. I was sliding my arms into my jacket sleeves when McKenna commented, "I knew something was going on with you and Kenan."

I willed the heat in my cheeks away, knowing the effort was futile. I hoped she didn't notice my blush when I glanced over and asked, "What are you talking about?"

McKenna's eyes, so similar to Kenan's even though they were a different color, held a sly glint. "You don't have to admit anything, but I'm not stupid. I'll just badger Kenan for it."

She noticed the look on my face. "I'm just kidding," she said quickly.

McKenna and I were friends. I suddenly wanted to confide everything to her. Yet it all felt like too much.

She studied me for several long moments before she added, "If you need to talk, I'm here."

# Chapter Twenty-Six

# KENAN

I'd seen Quinn come out of the pharmacy before I encountered her on the sidewalk. I tried to tell myself there were plenty of reasons for anyone to stop by the pharmacy. In Fireweed Harbor, the pharmacy wasn't just a pharmacy. It was a general store with odds and ends.

They even sold beer and wine there. Yet I couldn't ignore the niggling feeling that Quinn was keeping something from me. All of my suspicious curiosity looped back to that doctor's appointment in Juneau.

A few days later, we were having dinner—something we'd done once or twice a week for the past few years. Now though, it felt different. There was before I'd kissed Quinn and after I'd kissed Quinn. I'd picked up pizza on the way over to her house. When she opened the door for me, I found myself leaning down to kiss her. Because I couldn't help it. Her eyes were bright, and her lips were pink and full.

I was a little breathless when I lifted my head a moment later. Her cheeks were flushed. Her dog Bela trotted over and wiggled in a circle around us.

"Hey," Quinn said.

I was relieved she sounded as breathless as I felt. I cleared my throat. "Hey." I lifted the pizza a little higher. "I got two boxes."

"I can count," she said dryly as she closed the door behind me. "I swung by The Sugar Spoon and got your favorite chocolate mousse cheesecake," she added.

We walked together toward the kitchen area. "A woman after my heart," I commented as I set the pizzas on the counter.

That would normally be just a one-off teasing response to her. But just now, my heart kicked hard in response with the beat echoing through my body. Everything felt imbued with more meaning with her.

"I also picked up some of the fresh spiced apple pie beer and mead. We have choices," she said as she waggled her eyebrows.

I took a steadying breath. I had to remind myself to act normal. I was the one who'd suggested we see where things went. And, here I was, starting to panic about it.

I craved a distraction. I knew just the one.

Quinn's kitchen had a low section of the counter. She told me it was for baking. She had started to turn and walk toward the refrigerator. I reached out, catching her lightly by the elbow. She spun back, and I reeled her closer to me.

"What is it?" she asked, stopping inches away from me.

*"This."* I bent low and fit my mouth over hers, claiming her with a deep kiss. My desire pounded so rapidly inside me that I could hardly think through the drumbeat of it.

Our kiss started deep as I swept my tongue into her mouth, breathing her in, needing her as much as I needed air. The moment I tasted her, everything slowed. It was as if a curtain fell around us, catching us in a shimmer of sparks.

Our kiss gentled, our tongues lazily teasing. I drew back, resting my forehead on hers.

"Quinn," I whispered against her lips.

"Kenan."

I felt the sound of her saying my name in my heart. I had one hand cupping her nape, and the other palming her cheek. I felt as if my heart had been kicked over and lay sprawled and stunned before her. I was enthralled—to her, to this woman who was my best friend. Everything with her was startling in its intensity. Instead of this fiery-hot chemistry beginning to cool, it was heating up with the flames licking higher and higher, the fire white hot.

She made an impatient sound in the back of her throat, just a little hitch, something between a whimper and a sigh.

A second later, we kissed again. I needed her with a fierceness and desperation that shocked me. The next few moments were a messy fumble. Only half of our clothes were off, my jeans were shoved down around my hips, and hers were tossed to the floor. I lifted her onto that low counter, remembering a condom at the last minute and smoothing it on before I teased my fingers into her slippery wet core, growling to find her slick with arousal.

On the heels of a deep breath, I sank inside her. It felt like coming home when I joined with her like this. I seated myself deeply, nudging once when I was fully inside her. Her blouse was unbuttoned, and I could feel her nipples through the lace of her bra pressing against my chest.

I sucked in a ragged breath, opening my eyes. Hers

were closed, and her lips were pink and kiss-swollen. Her cheeks were flushed. I could feel the rapid beat of her heart, a wild tumble, just like mine.

"Quinn, I want to see you. Look at me," I rasped.

Her lashes lifted. Her hazel gaze was dark, the green standing out, a tiny detail I noticed whenever she was aroused.

We held still like that, caught in that shimmer of sparks. The moment felt suspended, slow, intimate, and so intense I could hardly breathe through the emotion rushing through me. I could feel my heartbeat in my cock as I drew back and filled her again, the very heart of her rippling and clenching around me.

I watched as her eyes held mine. She bit her lip at one point, letting out a little sigh before she whispered, "Kenan, please."

I knew her torch song now, knew she was building to her crescendo. She blinked, and her legs tightened around my hips as I filled her once more. I reached between us, teasing my fingers over her slippery and swollen clit.

Her sharp cry rang out when she came, her hips bucking into me as I filled her once more. I finally let my release take hold, its claws sinking deep as I shuddered with her.

She tucked her head in the curve of my neck. I held her close as my heart thundered and the reality of what was happening slammed into me. I'd gone and fallen in love with my best friend.

For several heart-stopping seconds, a sense of panic struck me. But this was Quinn. Above all, she was my friend. I just needed not to panic. I needed to wait. To make sure she felt the same way and I wasn't going to screw this all up.

# Chapter Twenty-Seven

# KENAN

In hindsight, I supposed it was a good thing we had that quick and dirty encounter in the kitchen. At the very least, it relieved the constant buzz of need I experienced with Quinn. I was less on edge, less tense.

It was late, coming up on when I would generally get ready to leave. I didn't want to leave. I wanted to sleep here, and not because I wanted sex. I just wanted to be close to Quinn.

This was the part where I might've fucked up. Because I was nervous and deeply unsettled by my feelings. I told her I needed to go to the bathroom. I did, but I needed a minute to figure out how the hell to say to her I just wanted to stay the night.

While she put things away in the kitchen, I went to the bathroom. As I washed my hands in the sink, my eyes landed on a medication bottle. She'd left it out. If it was a secret, she wouldn't leave it there.

That was what I told myself. I lifted the bottle, noting the date of the prescription. It was the same day I'd seen her on the sidewalk by the pharmacy. I pulled up the medication on my phone. What the fuck?

I still had the medication in my hand when I walked out to the kitchen. I wasn't thinking at all.

"What the hell is this?" I barked as I walked straight up to her.

Quinn was drying her hands on a dish towel and turned to face me. Her jaw went a little slack. "None of your business!" She tossed the dish towel on the counter and held her hand out. "Give me that."

"Are you okay? And why are you taking fertility medication?"

She looked distinctly uncomfortable. I handed the medication over, waiting with tension drawn tight inside.

"I'm trying to get pregnant," she finally said. "I want to have a baby. This whole process started before"—she flapped her hand in the air—"this thing with you happened."

"And you weren't going to tell me? Why didn't you tell me before?"

"Because. My luck in dating isn't good. You know that. I'm not getting any younger. I knew if I wanted to have a baby, I should look into the process sooner rather than later. I didn't tell anyone about it except my doctor. Because it's private, and I don't know if it'll work. I preferred to keep it to myself." Her tone was pointed and her eyes narrowed as we had a stare down.

"Well, even if we weren't having this thing, you could've asked me."

"Asked you what?" Her voice rose sharply.

"If you're going to have a baby, you might as well have a baby with someone you know rather than some random stranger."

"You've always told me you never wanted kids."

Okay, that was true, but I didn't even want to go there with that right now. I clenched and stretched my jaw open as I spun away, stuffing my hands in my pockets. I paced from the kitchen into the living room and back again. "I just feel like you're hiding something pretty important from me. Was this what that appointment was about in Juneau?"

She swallowed and nodded. "I didn't feel like telling you about it. I'm sorry if that hurts your feelings. Do you suddenly want kids?"

We stared at each other. Removing my hands from my pockets, I dragged a palm across my cheek in a reflexive, nervous gesture. I distantly noted I was due for a shave.

"I don't know," I said with a shrug.

Quinn set the medication bottle on the counter. "I don't want to argue about this, Kenan."

I closed my eyes, taking a deep breath. When I opened them, I felt a little calmer. "I don't either. I guess it just freaked me out. You're my best friend."

"You're my best friend too. Can we just put this on ice for now?"

I nodded. "Can I stay tonight?"

She turned back, her eyes widening in surprise. "The night?"

"Yes."

We studied each other for a long moment. I held my breath until she nodded. "Of course."

This wasn't the first time we slept together. We'd spent two nights together on the ferry and another in the hotel. Yet those were all outside of Fireweed Harbor. Somehow, spending the night in her bedroom and in her house felt different. It felt like we took things to another level because this was part of our regular lives. This was where we lived; it was our world.

The following morning, I ignored the doubts competing for my attention. I didn't want to think about Quinn doing IVF treatment and potentially getting inseminated with some random stranger's genetic material. I just couldn't even go there.

I kissed her when we woke up together. One kiss led to another. I tugged her into the shower with me and made love to her against the tiled wall. I told myself it was just sex, but my heart knew the truth. When we parted ways, we pretended our argument didn't linger between us.

# Chapter Twenty-Eight

# QUINN

Later that afternoon, I left my office. I told Rhys I was meeting at our family's offices because my father had questions about a contract. My father was mostly retired and didn't have questions about anything. These days, he did, as he described it, the fun stuff— real estate transactions, weird fishing rights issues, and more. I just needed to get out of my office.

My feet moved in the direction of Spill the Beans Café. Maybe an afternoon dose of caffeine would clear my thoughts. I still couldn't get over the look of hurt on Kenan's face when he realized I hadn't told him something. I felt guilty even though I knew I had every right not to tell him everything. I hadn't discussed my choice to look into IVF with anyone because I didn't know how it would go.

My heart was still tripping and stumbling over him. What if he maybe wanted kids? What if it was something we could do together? Those were treacherous questions to contemplate.

A few minutes later, I stood at the counter in the

café, and Phyllis smiled over at me. It was midafternoon, a quieter time of day here. "What will it be?"

"I'll just take your bold brew."

She got a cup ready for me and handed it over. "Anything to eat?"

I hadn't even eaten lunch. As if my stomach wanted to answer her, it growled audibly.

Phyllis waggled her brows. "We've got our soup of the day. Today is a salmon bisque. It's delicious."

"I'll take a bowl of that with some of your bread."

"I'm hungry too. Why don't I join you?" she asked.

A few minutes later, we sat together at a small table by the windows. She had called out Heather, their newest employee, a girl from high school covering the afternoons, to handle customers. Heather was drawing a Christmas tree in the corner of the chalkboard behind the register counter.

"Now, let's get right down to it," Phyllis said after we had both taken a few spoonfuls of soup.

"Get down to what?"

Her brows hitched up. "Something is on your mind. You are probably the least distracted person I know, and you look really distracted. I might even go so far as to say you look worried."

"Phyllis, I'm fine," I insisted.

She tsk-tsked me. "I've known you since you were a baby. Now just tell me the truth."

I took a deep breath, realizing Phyllis would be safe to confide in. She could be gossipy but only traded in superficial details that wouldn't hurt anyone.

"You are sworn to secrecy before I say a word," I said, pointing my finger at her.

Phyllis made the sign of the cross over her chest. "Cross my heart."

"Okay..." I quickly spilled the whole story, ending

with, "I just figured I have the shittiest luck with relationships, and I don't want to wait forever. I also don't want to end up in one of those relationships where I'm doing all the work anyway. Then this whole thing started with Kenan, and I'm pretty sure it's a mistake. He's always said he didn't want kids, and he never even wanted to get serious. It's not like I don't understand where he's coming from." I let out a sigh.

Phyllis interjected, "Things weren't great for them as kids. Their mother is wonderful, but their father died young, and I think she was overwhelmed. Her plate was full, and she didn't know what was going on. To this day, I know she wishes their father was still here. So many things would've been different if he hadn't passed away."

I nodded. "I know. I think—" My words cut off abruptly.

Because I didn't really know what to think. I knew Kenan was hurt, but he had told me time and time again he didn't want a family.

"I think there's what Kenan thinks in his head." She tapped her temple. "And then his emotions. I've seen him with his nephew. He's incredible with him." She was referring to the unexpected nephew they'd gained when an ex of Jake's showed up with his son. When paternity testing confirmed his parenthood, Kenan had been great with him, easygoing and supportive, easing his entrance into their family.

I thought about Kenan's messy family. There was a lot of love among the siblings, and their bond with their mother had strengthened since the whole sordid story about all that had happened with their grandfather came out. Kenan had told me he barely remembered his father. He had been so young when he passed that memories were faint.

I knew he carried guilt, feeling like Jake and Rhys bore the brunt of the abusive behavior of their grandfather. I understood why Kenan said he would be the best uncle ever, but that was enough for him.

These thoughts tumbled through my mind while I sipped my coffee. Phyllis studied me quietly.

Eventually, she said, "I think Kenan's afraid. I think he's always been afraid of falling in love. That's why he and Blake share that tendency to keep things light. But I also think he's afraid of really seeing all that he could be. For better or worse, when you're in a big group of siblings like his, getting lost in the shuffle can be easy. I don't think he's lost, but he's not sure what his role is. After Jake died, Rhys stepped up to be the eldest brother and took care of everything. Blake runs the production and distribution. Adam, as close as he and Kenan are, is considered the brainiest. I don't know that that's true, just that he's really good at math. Kenan is just as smart as Adam is but in a different way. He's the creative one who thinks on the fly and solves problems. I'm not saying I know what you want, but I think you should give Kenan a chance. You know as well as I do that, given the chance, he would make a very good father and a good partner to anyone. That man is as loyal as they come. You have to believe he can rise to the challenge. I want to convince you that he will, but you have to believe in yourself. You also have to know what's in your own heart. I had a good marriage, but it wasn't perfect. Anyone who tells you their marriage was perfect is lying through their teeth, by the way."

I snorted at that. "I appreciate your honesty, Phyllis."

Just then, Hazel came in from the back, calling over, "I heard that!" She approached our table, nodding vigorously. "There's a reason we're best friends and have been since college. She knows I miss my George," she said, referring to her late husband, "but Lord knows it wasn't perfect. If he rose from the dead, I'm certain we would argue about something. No matter how much I missed him, that man could drive me nuts. Are you telling Quinn she should give Kenan a chance?"

Heat flashed into my cheeks. I was about to ask her what she knew when Hazel added, "I don't know anything, but I've seen you two together for years. We always thought you'd make a good couple."

"We?!" I squeaked. "Is this something you've talked about?"

Hazel rolled her eyes. "Of course. Plus, I saw his hand on your knee the other day when you were here together."

Phyllis glanced up at her. "It's complicated. Quinn wants to have a baby. Kenan has said for years he didn't want kids. He's going to have to figure out he can do both, and she's going to have to believe it."

"Oh my God," I muttered.

Hazel studied me, her gaze kind. "It's never simple. Here's the funny thing. Some people plan to have babies, then have one and break up because it's not what they expected. Neither one of us had kids because we didn't want them. Sometimes I wonder about it, but I'm old enough now that I've accepted my choice. Kenan is a good man. No matter what you do, life is complicated and messy, and things change all the time. Just tell him how you feel and see what happens."

"How I feel?"

"Well, you love him, don't you?"

My heart carried on beating, strong and steady. I

glanced between Phyllis and Hazel. I'd known them for as long as I could remember. They'd opened this coffee shop together after college.

"I'm just going to have to think about what to do," I finally said, even though I knew I loved him.

I just wasn't ready to say it out loud. When I did say it out loud, I also knew it had to be to Kenan. If I ever scrambled up the nerve.

# Chapter Twenty-Nine

# KENAN

"Hey, hey," Blake said as I walked into the kitchen at our mother's house.

I grinned over at him. "Hey, yourself." His step-daughter, Lia, stood on a stool with an apron with a cat on it tied around her waist as she peered into a mixing bowl and stirred with a giant wooden spoon.

I stopped beside her. "What are you making there?" I asked as I slid an arm around her shoulders and squeezed lightly.

"Cookies." She looked up at me. "It's hard to stir them." Her brow crinkled with her concentration as she glanced back down.

"I have just the trick." I turned and walked into my mother's pantry. A moment later, I carried out her stand mixer, which was tucked in a corner.

Blake looked from the mixer to Lia to me. "Didn't even know Mom had that."

"That's because I pay better attention than you," I quipped.

Lia smiled at me, asking, "What's that?"

"A stand mixer. I promise it'll change your life."

A few minutes later, after I had it set up and helped her move the dough into the mixer bowl, I showed her how to work it.

She squealed with glee when the cookie dough was thoroughly mixed so quickly. "You're the best!"

"I thought I was the best," Blake teased as I helped her scoop spoonfuls of cookie dough onto a baking tray. He met my gaze over the top of her head and winked.

My heart gave a funny beat in my chest as my mind spun to my conversation with Quinn. I *had* said I didn't want kids, but it wasn't that specifically. Family was incredibly important to me. Yet I had always carried this deep fear that I wouldn't be enough.

A little while later, our mother helped Lia check the cookies in the oven. Blake and I sat at the kitchen table, the very table where we often had dinners together as kids. Our grandfather had never lived here. Thank fucking God, or it would've ruined the good memories I had. This was our sanctuary.

I glanced over at Blake, considering him for a moment. "What?" he prompted as he took a swallow of water.

"Just thinking. Being a father suits you. Did you expect it to be so easy?"

"Fuck no!" he retorted quickly. "You know as well as I do that I didn't ever plan to settle down. I didn't think it was for me." He paused, his gaze shifting to Lia for a long moment. An intense emotion flickered in his eyes when he brought his attention back to me. "It's both easier and more difficult than I expected. The love and the commitment and, frankly, the day-to-day shit is the easiest part. The hard part is realizing that you carry the weight of just how much they matter. If something happened to Fiona or Lia, I don't know what I would do. It might break me at this point. Why do you ask?"

Although Adam and I were the closest, Blake and I had our own special bond. That was the funny part about being in a cluster of siblings. You had different connections with each of them. For whatever reason, Blake and I shared the role of kind of being the jokers in the family, the ones to smooth things over and snap through a difficult moment with a joke and a laugh. As a result, we also shared the understanding that not everybody took us seriously.

Rhys carried the mantle of being the oldest sibling and the one expected to step into a leadership role. That had never sat well for Jake. He'd always seemed as if he wanted to shake it off. Rhys accepted the role without hesitation, and it suited him. I knew Blake knew about me and Quinn, at least part of us. I hadn't admitted to anyone, barely even myself, that I was in love with her. As hurt as I was by the secret she'd kept from me, I knew I couldn't talk to anyone about it. That was hers.

"I don't know," I finally said. "Things are, uh, I guess, feeling complicated with Quinn. I'm worried I might've screwed things up."

"Don't count yourself out," Blake said, his gaze entirely serious as he leaned forward and rested his elbows on the table. "You're more than you give yourself credit for. We all have our reasons for being gunshy about relationships. I'm starting to realize maybe what we all went through only made us stronger. Everybody's got something to carry. I said it before, and I'll say it again: even when you were swearing up and down there would never be anything between you and Quinn, I knew you'd make a good couple. Really good. I just think you need to give yourself a chance, as much as her."

His words slammed into me so hard it felt as if he'd thumped me right in the chest. The sensation reverberated in my solar plexus.

Lia approached the table, stopping beside me. "You first," she said, holding the plate aloft.

"Ooh, I'm the lucky one today."

Blake chuckled. "How come I'm not first?" he teased.

"Because you didn't know where the stand mixer was," Lia replied with a sly grin.

As soon as I took a cookie off the plate, she rounded the table to Blake. He curled his arms around her shoulders, hugging her close as he dropped a kiss on top of her head. "It's a good thing Kenan knew where that mixer was. Now we know for the future."

"Can we get one at home?" Lia asked.

Blake chuckled as he lifted a cookie off. "Definitely. I can't believe I didn't think of that sooner."

"Well, you're not a chef like Mom," she pointed out.

I took a bite of the cookie. It was warm, and the texture was just perfect. I let out a moan, chewing before offering, "These are amazing, Lia. You take after your mom."

Fiona happened to walk into the kitchen, glancing over at the table. "I'm not that great at baking. I'm decent, but it's definitely not my strength."

"I'm going to be the baker in the family," Lia announced.

There was a sense of comfort and warmth whenever I was with my siblings. I wondered if I wanted that for myself. The tricky thing was, if I could imagine it with anyone, it would be with Quinn.

Now, I just had to convince her.

# Chapter Thirty

# QUINN

I idly studied the medication bottle, contemplating when I wanted to start taking them. After that, I walked into my kitchen, sliding my hips onto a stool by the counter and tapping my phone screen. I had a list of profiles to review, potential mystery fathers for a potential mystery child-to-be.

Every time I logged in to the system to review these, I would only read for a few minutes before logging out, which was exactly what happened again.

"Fuck you, Kenan," I whispered.

This was all his fault. He'd gone and proposed I give him a chance to be the father. Now, he made me want things I'd already let go of. It seemed like such a high bar to find happily ever after with some guy who wasn't a jerk, some guy where it didn't mean sex was a total letdown. I knew Kenan had it in him to be an amazing father, but I didn't think he believed it, so it wouldn't come to be.

The worst part of it all was I loved him. It terrified me because it would be easier to imagine doing this parenting thing with him just as friends because then I wouldn't expect more. I wouldn't want more.

I set my phone down, leaning my face into my hands and letting out a groan. My eyes pricked with tears, but I refused to give in to them. I wasn't going to get through this by crying over it.

I'd walked into this mess myself. I could walk myself out of it. I straightened and let my hands fall to the counter.

Now, I wanted more. I wanted Kenan and the whole package.

# Chapter Thirty-One

# QUINN

Wednesday rolled around, and Kenan texted me.

**Kenan:** *Locals' night at the winery tonight?*

I studied that text for *way* too long. We'd probably sent the same text to each other hundreds of times before. Nothing about it was remarkable. I didn't doubt that hundreds of friends in our small town sent some variation of the same text. Locals' night at Fireweed Winery was a favorite local event.

Kenan and I often met there. It was casual and easy, and many of our friends would be there.

I took a slow breath, willing my heartbeat, which was galloping out of control, to slow the hell down. This was no big deal. I lifted my phone and tapped out my reply.

**Me:** *Sure. Meet you there.*

I set my phone down, telling myself to focus on work. I always had plenty to do. Maybe a minute had passed when my phone vibrated. I told myself I didn't have to look right away, but I was already reaching for my phone. Sliding it closer, I tapped on the screen.

**Kenan:** *I'll meet you at the office. I'll be by at the end of*

*the day anyway. I have to check in with Rhys about
something.*

**Me:** *OK. See you when you get here.*

This time, I silenced my phone. I didn't need to
wonder when he might text again. I even tucked my
phone into my purse and zipped the side pocket shut
for good measure. These were the measures I was
taking to inoculate myself against the temptation to
see when Kenan might text again.

We hadn't discussed it, and I doubted we ever
would, but our old habit of occasionally texting each
other silly memes during the day had stopped. I
missed it. It felt like we were being too careful with
each other. Another reminder that maybe this was all a
huge, heartbreaking mistake.

It was later in the day, late enough that Kenan was
probably somewhere in the building. He didn't have a
regular schedule. Rhys was prone to show up early and
stay late. Although his schedule was a little better
since he had fallen in love.

Kenan had a fairly unorthodox schedule. He
worked a lot, but in his role as the catchall for odds
and ends, he might be out at the garage handling
equipment issues for the business, stopping by the
winery to check in with Blake about matters at the
distribution warehouse, or coming in to the actual
office.

I'd never wondered what he did during the days.
I did now. I wondered why he was stopping by to
meet with Rhys. Although we coordinated when
needed, I didn't know everything he did. Lately, I
wondered what he was doing all the freaking time.

When might I see him again? That was *always* the question.

I saved a document on my computer and made a quick phone call to my mother. She had asked me to look at the schedule for a trip she wanted to plan for her and my father. She was giving him a surprise trip for his birthday. They were going to take a cruise from Alaska down to the coast of Mexico.

She answered on the first ring. "Hi, Quinn!"

"Hey, Mom. Just following up. I looked at the schedule you sent and think it looks great. Dad will love it. Do you all need me to cover anything while you're gone?"

I could hear the smile in her voice when she replied, "I'm sure your dad will fuss about it, but as it is, we're not working full-time now. We can dial back. Danielle will field anything that comes up in a pinch. I'm sure your father will want you to say that you'll cover anything that comes up, so be prepared to do that. I've got it all set so you won't need to do a thing."

I laughed softly. "Mom, you know I don't mind."

"I know, but you work enough as it is. You handle the most challenging part of our practice at Fireweed Industries."

"So when is this trip happening?"

"In March. I figure we'll both be sick of winter by then. Mud season will be coming up. Speaking of winter, we're doing Thanksgiving with the Cannons this year, as usual."

A sense of anxiety tightened inside. We usually did Thanksgiving with the Cannons. There was absolutely nothing out of the ordinary about that. Except *every-thing* felt loaded with Kenan.

"I assumed," I replied lightly. "Is Thanksgiving already upon us?" I glanced at my desk calendar, my brain noting that it was next Thursday. "Are we doing the tree at the house on the Friday after?"

That was another tradition. My mother liked to decorate the tree the day after Thanksgiving. Ever since I was a little girl, we decorated a tall blue spruce tree in my parents' front yard.

"Of course. Although, I was going to ask you if you thought Kenan wouldn't mind coming to help," she replied.

"I'm sure he'll help. Is everything okay?"

My mother's soft sigh filtered through the line. "Well, your father is not as young as he once was. I'm a little worried about him getting up on the ladder to do all those lights. If Kenan could help, I'd love it."

"Of course. That makes sense. Dad's probably going to have an opinion about that, you know."

"Just have Kenan come over. We won't make it a thing, and Kenan can help," she insisted.

"Because denial is always helpful," I teased.

"Thanks for asking Kenan. He's a tactful man."

"Are you going to locals' night tonight?" I asked.

"I'm not sure. We'll see."

"Well, if you're there, I'll be there. Love you, Mom."

We ended our call, and I tucked my phone back into my purse. I stood and headed to the bathroom before I got ready to leave. My office was a few doors down from Rhys's. As I approached his door, I saw it was slightly ajar and heard Kenan's voice. I would've recognized it anyway, but now, when I heard the sound of it, my pulse lunged ahead.

I wasn't eavesdropping, not on purpose. Or that was what I tried to tell myself as my footsteps slowed. Rhys asked, "Well, how do you feel about it?"

"I don't know," Kenan replied with an unsteady

sigh. I could practically picture him running his hand through his hair. "I just don't know if I'm ready. I'm afraid I'll fuck it up."

My stride quickened, and I couldn't get past that doorway fast enough into the bathroom. All the while, I was trying to walk quietly so no one noticed I was in the hallway. Kenan had to be talking about us.

# Chapter Thirty-Two

# KENAN

"Hey, Mom," I said as I leaned over and kissed her on the cheek.

She smiled up at me and slid her hand through my elbow and squeezed. "Hi, dear. How are you?"

"Pretty good. And you?"

My mother squeezed my elbow again. "I'm going to Seattle for the weekend. Cathy has a work trip there, and I'll be able to see Matthew for the whole weekend."

Matthew was our surprise nephew, the one none of us knew about. Cathy had dated or rather had a situationship with Jake and Rhys in college. She hadn't told anyone she got pregnant. Jake was the father. She would probably never admit it, but we all presumed she eventually found out our family had money and decided to come clean.

For our mother, it was bittersweet. Matthew looked so much like Jake. Cathy lived in California and brought Matthew up at least once a year. Our mother tried to visit several times a year.

"That is excellent. Give him a big hug from Uncle Kenan," I replied.

My mother chuckled and released my elbow after one more squeeze. She was instantly drawn into a conversation with the town's police chief, Mike, and Fiona's mother. As far as I could tell, they were dating and trying to pretend they weren't.

Blake appeared at my side, clapping me on the shoulder. "Hey, man, how's it going?"

"Pretty good. Is Fiona in the kitchen tonight?"

His eyes were warm as he nodded. "Of course."

Lia appeared hand in hand with Haven. As soon as she saw me, she dropped Haven's hand and launched at me. I caught her in my arms and lifted her high in the air, giving her a quick spin before setting her back on the ground. "Hey, Miss Lia! Are you all having dinner tonight?"

Lia nodded. "And Blake's driving, so he can't have anything to drink."

Blake chuckled as Haven grinned down at her before looking toward me and offering, "Hey, Kenan."

I dipped my chin in acknowledgment. "Is he allowed to have water?" I asked as I looked back down at Lia.

She contemplated this as she tapped her toe on the floor and rested a hand on her hip. "Yes," she announced after a moment.

Just then, I felt a prickle race up my spine. I didn't even know how I knew, but I knew Quinn had just approached. We had walked over together a few minutes earlier. She had seemed a little off. I wanted to chalk it up to our argument, but it felt like something more.

Haven was saying something. "I was just dropping Lia off. Rhys and I are headed home. Our babysitter needs to go home soon. I'm going to walk over to meet him at his office. Good night, all," she said with a wave.

I waved just as Quinn stopped beside me. "Hey again," I said, smiling down at her. My heart kicked a little faster against my ribs. When she smiled, it didn't quite reach her eyes. "Is everything okay?" I asked.

"Of course," she said quickly.

I wanted to press, but Blake interjected, and Adam appeared. The conversation carried on, and I managed to hold up my end. I let my gaze drift around the space. Christmas decorations were up with lights strung above the bar, and clusters of spruce boughs with bright red bows were mounted in intervals on the walls. Locals' night next week would be an early Thanksgiving for the town. We coordinated with a local nonprofit to offer a free dinner earlier in the day to families in need and gave away turkeys until they ran out.

My mother had mentioned we were having Thanksgiving with Quinn's family. Our families had had Thanksgiving together since we were little kids, so it was nothing unusual. But lately, everything with Quinn had a new thread of tension woven through it. My mind spun back to my conversation about an hour ago with Rhys. I had confided in him that Quinn wanted to have a baby. I even admitted to falling in love with Quinn, but I was afraid I couldn't be the one she needed.

He told me it was never simple and that he had more faith in me than I had in myself.

At some point during the hour or so that I was there, a group of us went into the restaurant for dinner. I sat beside Adam, with Quinn on my other side. While eating, a casual friend, Melanie, paused by the table. Melanie had grown up in Fireweed Harbor. She and I had something like a friends-with-benefits arrangement for a while, but it had petered out when it became clear she wanted something more.

She'd been the one to break it off. She was happily engaged now and expecting a baby.

"When's the baby due?" Tessa asked with a wink as she smiled over at her.

"Three months. I still can't believe how fast the time has gone by." Melanie smoothed her hand over her belly.

"Here's hoping the rest of your pregnancy remains uneventful," Tessa said as she held up her bottle of mead, toasting Melanie in the air.

Melanie smiled. "Thank you."

It was a nothing interaction, or so I thought. Until I glanced down and saw the look in Quinn's eyes. Her mouth was tight at the corners, and something about her gaze was almost wistful.

———

*Thanksgiving Day*

"I'm so full!" McKenna said as she closed the dishwasher.

"Isn't that expected on Thanksgiving?" Rhys teased. He hung the dish towel over the oven door handle before turning and leaning his hips against the counter.

"Definitely expected," I replied.

The hum of voices from the dining room at my mother's house carried into the kitchen. I glanced around, experiencing a sense of warmth. All my siblings were here, and it felt good to be together. My eyes were drawn toward the archway between the kitchen and dining area when Quinn walked past, disappearing down the hallway. I presumed she was going to the bathroom.

I wasn't thinking when I turned and followed her as McKenna said something to Griffin. The doorway to the bathroom down that hall was closed. I waited across from it, stuffing my hands in my pockets and leaning my head against the wall.

As soon as I heard the toilet flush and the water running in the sink, my heart started pounding in anticipation. Quinn had been here for hours with her parents, and we hadn't had a second alone.

She stepped out of the bathroom, her eyes widening when she saw me. "Hey," I said.

"Hey." Her eyes darted down the hallway toward the dining room.

"Don't worry. Just wondering if I can come over tonight."

I saw her shoulders rise as she took a quick breath in. "Sure."

"Great, then I'll see you later."

She started to walk down the hall before turning back quickly. "My mom wants to know if you can come over tomorrow when we hang the lights on the tree in front of my parents' house. She's worried about my dad getting on the ladder." Quinn's lips twisted to the side with a wry smile. "She somehow wants it to be all casual so my dad doesn't notice that you're doing all the work on the ladder."

I chuckled. "Understood. Of course I'll help. What time should I plan to go over?"

"We usually do it in the afternoon. Maybe three?"

"I'll be there."

I wanted to pull her close and kiss her, but I knew that wouldn't fly. Anybody could come down this hallway at any second.

"I'll see you later," I said, keeping my tone low.

She nodded before she whisked away, hurrying down the short hallway and disappearing out of sight.

# Chapter Thirty-Three

# QUINN

I absolutely shouldn't have had another night with Kenan. I wanted far too much, and I didn't know what to do about it. Despite the doubts bouncing around in my mind, I savored every second with him, especially the mornings.

Waking up with Kenan was a special kind of heaven. He was warm and strong. I loved when he curled around me. I woke up, feeling his muscled chest against my shoulder blades and the subtle crinkly feel of his chest hair against my skin. Not once in my life had I ever thought about the way a man's chest hair felt.

Kenan was almost sweetly sensual in the morning. He would kiss me lazily, sometimes he would tease me to a climax in bed, and other times we would shower together.

This morning, he'd offered to make breakfast, pointing out that it was the day after Thanksgiving and almost everything was closed. He made me waffles and bacon. I told myself I needed to tell him I had something to do so we didn't spend the whole day together before we went to my parents' house. Except I didn't want him to leave.

Hours later, Kenan tactfully handled all of the lights on the upper portion of the tree in the yard. My heart twisted in my chest when I looked up, and he called down to my father, "Like this?"

If my father noticed that Kenan took over all the ladder work for the day, he went along with it because Kenan made it easy. It was all good. I still kept turning over in my mind the conversation I'd overheard in Rhys's office.

Kenan drove me back to my place. When he stopped in the front, he turned off his car and glanced over. "Can I come in?"

"Of course." A sense of trepidation slipped through me. I didn't know what was on his mind, but it seemed like he wanted to talk.

When we got inside, I asked if he wanted any leftovers. As our families usually did, we had divvied up the leftovers from Thanksgiving. There was always more than enough to go around.

Kenan shook his head. "Thanks for asking, but I'm still full from the turkey sandwiches your mom made." He leaned his hands on the counter, his eyes on mine.

"What is it?" I asked. My belly wobbled with anxiety.

He pressed his tongue into the side of his cheek, his eyes dipping down to the counter and then back up. "Let me be the one."

"Huh?"

"Let's do this for real. We were already going to see how things work for us. If you really want to have a baby, I want to be the father."

"Wha-a-a-t?" I sputtered.

Something flickered in his eyes, but he straightened, lifted his chin, and squared his shoulders. "Let me be the one. For you. For our baby. I love you, Quinn."

My pulse stuttered, and then my heart felt as if it was soaring skyward with a rush of joy, almost like a thunderclap inside of my chest.

I still couldn't catch up. "Are you... are you—" I stuttered again before forcing myself to pause and take a slow breath. "Kenan, I love you too, but I don't want you to do something you never wanted to do just because I want it. That seems like a recipe for disaster. I don't handle a lot of family law, but you know my cousin does. There's nothing worse than people going along with having a kid when they don't want one."

Kenan held my gaze for a long moment. "Quinn, I've thought about this. I promise you. I want this. With you."

I didn't realize I was shaking my head until he pushed back from the counter, jamming his hands in his pockets. "Wow. You have that little fucking faith in me. You know what? Let's forget about this before we make it worse. If you ever think you can believe in me, let me know."

Panic started to churn inside as he turned and began to leave. "Kenan!" I called.

He turned back. "Yeah?"

"Can we just talk? I just, I don't, I don't think you're ready for this."

His eyes shuttered, and then he was gone. I didn't try to stop him.

For hours that night after he left, I kept picking up my phone and contemplating what I could say. I never mustered up the courage to call or text. I also kept praying he would call me and say that he had overreacted and knew we needed a little more time. Right?

He never called. The weekend passed with radio silence between us.

I went into the office early Monday, hoping to see him there. His office was dark.

At some point later in the morning, I had to check with Rhys about something. I refused to ask him where Kenan was.

Finally, later in the afternoon, when there was still no sign of Kenan in the office, I asked Tish if she happened to know where he was. I played it off like I needed to ask him about something.

She looked up. "Yeah, he took an unexpected trip to Willow Brook with Blake. They're doing some planning for the production and distribution area there. Blake was going to go on his own, but Kenan offered to go with him. You know those two. They're always better together."

"Oh," was all I could manage.

"I'm surprised he hasn't texted you about it," she said lightly.

I pasted a polite smile on my face and hoped it seemed normal. "Just a busy day and I lost track. I texted him, but if they were flying, he probably hasn't had a chance to reply yet." That was a total lie, but I didn't want to let on that something was amiss between us.

Her phone rang, and she took the call, giving me an apologetic smile.

I told myself that was for the best. Kenan was out of town for a few days. I didn't need to deal with running into him at work. We could get back to normal somehow.

Except I missed him. He wasn't texting me at all, and I hated it.

# KENAN

I leaned back into the couch cushions at Archer's house. My cousin glanced over with a tired smile. "It's good to sit down for a few minutes. Getting this place up and running has been a ton of work." Archer's gaze shifted to Blake as he sat beside me. "I have a lot of respect for what you've been handling."

Blake let out a dry chuckle. "I just picked up the reins of what was already established. You guys"—he gestured between Archer and Chase—"are doing all the stuff that was in place when I stepped in. On the upside, we won't have to spend a small fortune upgrading all the equipment like I did."

"David has been incredibly helpful," Archer said.

"Can we give him a bonus or something?" Chase asked.

"I already planned that for the end of the year," Blake replied. "He's traveled here a lot."

"It's a really good thing he's stepped down from handling chef duties," I said.

"I can't even imagine doing this without his help," Chase said.

"We're all grateful David found Fiona. If he wasn't happy with her, he would've insisted on continuing to run the kitchen at Fireweed Winery and somehow tried to help with this," I commented.

"How is Fiona?" Archer asked, addressing his question to Blake.

Blake's smile was warm. "She's great, really great."

I was getting accustomed to him being head over heels in love with Fiona, but I was still surprised at how easily he had adjusted. Like me, Blake had been committed to not being committed. Until Fiona.

I nudged Blake lightly with my elbow as I rolled my eyes. "She's doing a fantastic job with the restaurant. David's thrilled with her, and we all know how difficult he is to please when it comes to the kitchen at the restaurant. Blake can't really be objective because he's totally whipped."

Chase and Archer laughed just as Phoebe came through the front door. "Hey, guys!" she called over.

Archer stood and walked across the living room to meet her near the entryway. He gave her a lingering kiss. As they stepped apart, she glanced over. "There's pizza in the car. I forgot to bring it in."

"How many boxes?" I asked as I stood.

"Four large pizzas. There are four of you, so I figure maybe that'll be enough," she teased as she walked over.

Archer was opening the front door. "Do you need help?" I asked as I followed him over.

"There are groceries, too," Phoebe called from behind us.

Archer caught my eye. "Yes, please."

A while later, we were sitting in the living room with the pizza boxes on the coffee table as we all served ourselves. Phoebe had gone to take a shower.

"Is she still doing the hotshot firefighting thing?" I asked Archer as I selected a slice of pizza and slid it onto my plate.

He finished chewing a bite and nodded. "She just fills in sometimes. I know she loves it, but I worry. It's a risky job." His brow furrowed as he shrugged. "You know what I mean," he added, glancing at Chase.

Chase was also a hotshot firefighter. While he was picking up work with Fireweed Industries with Archer here, he still did on-call work for the local firefighter crew in town.

"Not gonna argue that it's a risky job," Chase said. "But you know Phoebe. She's as steady as you can get out in the field."

"I know," Archer said. "I'm trying not to tell her what to do."

"You know that won't work out," I offered with a chuckle. "Maybe I don't know Phoebe as well as you, but if you tell her what to do, she'll do the opposite."

Archer took a bite of his pizza. After another moment, he added, "She knows I worry, which is why she's only doing it on call."

We fell into an easy conversation, getting the update on Chase's new family. He had recently married and had a baby unexpectedly, but he seemed to have grabbed that chance with both hands.

At one point, he glanced over, addressing Blake, "So you're an instant stepfather. How are you feeling about that?"

Blake set his empty plate down and took a swallow from his beer. He looked thoughtful as he lowered the bottle. "If you had told me, even a few months before I met Fiona, that this would be my life, I would've laughed. But it doesn't freak me out at all. I love Fiona. Lia is part of the package. We're pretty fresh, so we're taking it on pace, but I'm ready."

"It's funny how that happens, isn't it?" Chase mused.

"That's one way to put it," I offered dryly as I glanced his way. "You didn't ever expect to see Hallie again and now you have a toddler with her. Kind of blows my mind."

"It still blows my mind," Chase replied with a chuckle. "But I wouldn't have it any other way."

I felt the tension tighten across my shoulders and shifted them to ease it away.

"What about you? Are you getting serious with anyone?" Archer prompted, his tone light and easy.

I opened my mouth to make light of it, but I couldn't even crack a joke. I felt his gaze on me and took a slow breath, trying to loosen the tension banded around my chest now.

"Hey, you okay?" Archer asked. "I kind of figured you'd say hell no, and that would be that."

I glanced from Blake to Archer to Chase, three men I trusted completely. "I kind of made a mess of things," I finally said.

"What happened?" Chase asked.

I leaned forward, resting my elbows on my knees as I tunneled my hands through my hair before straightening and letting them fall to my knees. "You guys know Quinn?"

"Of course," Archer replied. "She heads up the legal department for our main offices. You've gotten pretty tight since you both moved back to Fireweed Harbor."

With three pairs of gazes on me expectantly, I felt uncertain how to explain. Blake appeared to take pity on me and chimed in, "I asked him years ago if there was anything between him and Quinn. He swore up and down, backward, forward, and sideways, that there was no way, never, no how. I knew better. I would just like some credit for being right for once." Blake cuffed me playfully on the shoulder.

Chase chuckled. "Ah, I see. Are you worried you're going to mess your friendship up? Is that the issue?"

"Pretty sure I already fucked that up." I let out a sigh. "Here's the catch: she wants a family, and this is important to her, but I've told her for years I never wanted kids."

"So that's a deal-breaker?" Chase prompted.

"I don't want it to be," I said. "Honestly, it scares me. But when I think about it, it's something I want with her." I looked among them. "I love my family, all of you. But then—" I glanced at Blake. "Shit was fucked up for us. It's better now. We're all grown up, and we're all tight, but I worry."

Blake held my gaze steadily. "You'd make a great father," he said.

"But I don't think Quinn believes it. How do I convince her?"

As I looked around the room, Chase studied me. "For different reasons, my childhood was fucked up. I never wanted to get serious and thought I didn't want kids. Obviously, that changed. Now, I can't imagine life without my family."

"How do I convince Quinn I can do this?"

# Chapter Thirty-Five

# KENAN

The following morning, Chase had invited me over for coffee. Hallie handed me a mug, asking, "Do you want a bagel? We have fresh bagels, and I made some cream cheese with our smoked salmon left over from last summer."

"I can't say no to that," I teased. "Sounds amazing."

Hallie lifted her hands to tighten her ponytail, her hazel eyes twinkling with her smile. "It *is* good. I'll toast one for you with Chase's."

Chase came walking into the kitchen with their toddler sound asleep on his shoulder.

"How's Danny doing?" I took a swallow of my coffee as he sat down at the table across from me.

"Good. He's already played for over an hour, and now he's tired again," Chase said with a grin.

Hallie chuckled as she tapped the button on their toaster. A moment later, she handed Chase a mug of coffee, gesturing to the center of the table. "Cream is right there."

Chase grinned up at her, replying, "Thank you.

Now, lean down so I can kiss you. If I move too much, we'll wake Danny."

He gave her a lingering kiss when she bent down to meet him. Although my sibling relationship with Chase was newer because we had only discovered him a few years ago, I knew him well enough to know that this was a surprise. He was married with a child and content with his situation. He was a good guy, and I was happy for him and Hallie.

"Want to hold a sleeping almost three-year-old?" Chase asked. He reached with one hand to add some cream to his coffee, adding, "You become an expert at doing things with one hand after you have a baby."

I chuckled. "I'm sure you do. I'll take him if you'd like."

Chase took a swallow from his coffee, and then stood, carefully passing the sound asleep bundle of my nephew to me. Danny didn't even wake as I shifted him in my arms. He formed himself into a comma over my shoulder, entirely comfortable within a second or two.

Chase sat back down, removing the towel he'd laid over his shoulder. "Do I need that?" I asked.

He flashed a grin. "No. He's very routine. He usually wakes up raring to go. After running us ragged for an hour or so, he naps for a while."

Hallie approached the table with two plates with toasted bagels, setting them down and returning a moment later with a bowl of smoked salmon cream cheese as she sat down.

"You're not having one?" I prompted.

"I already had one. Do you want me to get yours ready?" She waggled her eyebrows as she gestured toward Danny on my shoulder.

I grinned. "I could test my skills at the one-handed

thing, but I'm not sure how I'm going to pull off getting the cream cheese on the bagel."

Hallie quickly spread cream cheese on both sides of the toasted bagel for me. After my first bite, I let out a satisfied moan. "That is some good smoked salmon."

"We smoked it ourselves," Chase said. "It's my dad's brining recipe. He swears by it. You know how it is in Alaska. Everybody has their expert recommendation. Do you guys smoke your own salmon?"

"We sure do. My mother has her own recipes. I'm always open to trying new things. Email me your recipe. Speaking of salmon, we should go dipnetting again next summer."

Chase nodded. "We always go. You just tell me when you'll be over this way, and we'll make it happen."

Dipnetting was a favorite local activity in Alaska. While it was lots of fun, it was a subsistence fishery for residents only. For some, the salmon got them through the winter with pounds and pounds of healthy, lean protein.

There were a few options of where to go in Alaska, and you had to pick one. Glancing at Chase, I asked, "Do you always do the Kenai River run?"

"I've done the China Poot fishery and the Kasilof River, but the salmon are the largest in the Kenai River, so it's my preference."

"Same here. I wish we could do them all, but since we have to pick one, that's my first choice," I agreed.

We finished eating, and Hallie left for work, leaving me and Chase at the house with Danny. "Do you all do daycare, or are you on duty today?"

"It's winter, so I don't have as much work, and she's busy with the holiday season. We mostly swap out schedules, but when we're both busy, we have family to help out."

Before Hallie left, they had put Danny down to finish his nap in the living room. He was within view of where we were seated in the kitchen.

"You seem to have settled right into this marriage and kid thing," I commented.

Chase chuckled, his gaze sobering. "You know, if you had asked me about it even a few months before this all went down, I would've told you no way, no how. But I love it. It helps that I love Hallie. Don't get me wrong, I was slightly terrified at the prospect when I found out she was pregnant and would keep the baby. I think things work out the way they're supposed to." He studied me for a moment. "I'm not saying you *should* have kids, but I think you'd make a good father. It sure seems like you love Quinn."

I took an unsteady breath. Anxiety slithered down my spine, and my heart tumbled unsteadily in my chest. I *did* love Quinn. I just didn't want to fail.

"I wish I knew what to do."

"Maybe it would help if you think about how you'd feel if you don't go for it," Chase suggested.

"What do you mean?"

"When I started to panic after I found out Hallie was having a baby and I was falling for her, sometimes I tried to imagine how I would feel if I didn't take the chance. That was more terrifying. How would you feel if Quinn had a baby on her own or if she was with someone else?"

I stared at Chase as a sense of panic seized me inside. "Oh fuck," I muttered.

"Didn't mean to scare you, but it's a way to think about any choice. You've obviously known Quinn longer than I knew Hallie before we were together. In the time we've been together, I've definitely learned that the underlying friendship is really fucking important. You don't just have to love each other; you have to like each other. Because the day-to-day shit can be hard. Life on its own can be hard. If you have someone you care about, and you're decent and there for each other when the logistic challenges of life slap you in the face, you're in a much better place. That's a foundation you can build on. Maybe I haven't known you forever, but I get the sense Quinn means a lot more to you than just a friend. Maybe thinking about it that way will help you figure out what you want."

After I left Chase's house, my mind kept spinning on that question. If I took the path that didn't include life with Quinn, a sense of bleakness gusted through me.

Maybe I had my answer, but I still wasn't sure Quinn had faith in me.

# Chapter Thirty-Six

# KENAN

Blake and I flew back to Fireweed Harbor, and I told myself I didn't have to rush this. As I drove into the office one morning, the holiday spirit was in full swing in Fireweed Harbor with holiday lights glittering in the snowy darkness. Quinn and I had seen each other once since I got back. We had played it off casually, like everything was fine with us. Except my heart ached and my pulse raced.

Every time I considered Chase's thought exercise, it nearly sent me into a panic. Because the idea of Quinn having a baby by herself—or even worse, actually meeting someone else and getting serious—was something I could hardly bear. My thoughts shied away from the idea like a wild pony.

Yet I was still smarting from the fact that I didn't feel like she believed in me enough to reconsider, to grow. Maybe I had been uncertain about being a father and taking that leap—not just with her but with anyone. She'd been so quick to dismiss me, saying she didn't think I was ready because of what I'd said before. It hurt a lot. I also wondered if she didn't have faith in me as a partner. That burned.

I stopped by Rhys's office one afternoon after he had texted me. When I popped in, Quinn stood beside his desk, holding a file folder against her chest. She looked over at me, smiling tightly. "Hey, Kenan," she said.

Her voice sounded casual, but I heard the underlying thread of tension woven into it.

"Hey," I replied.

She glanced back over at Rhys. "I'll follow up. I need to swing by to check in with my parents about something at their office. I'm sure I'll see you tomorrow."

"I'm sure you will," Rhys replied.

Quinn departed, closing Rhys's office door behind her. His gaze met mine—the look there far too perceptive for my comfort.

"What?" My tone was defensive, and I knew it.

"Nothing. Actually, I'm dodging there. I'll point out the obvious. Things seem a little tense between you and Quinn. Have you come to your senses yet?"

"What are you talking about?" I grumbled.

"You're in love with her. Just admit it and put the rest of us out of our misery."

I plunked down in the chair across from his desk with a sigh, running a hand through my hair before letting my hand fall with a thump to the armrest. "We're figuring it out."

"Are you? Because it seems like you're avoiding each other," he offered pointedly, although his tone was gentle.

I narrowed my eyes. "We're figuring it out," I repeated. "Now, what did you need?"

"Do you mind going to Juneau for two days? We're

going for it with setting up a smaller production warehouse there."

"I'll go. This afternoon?"

"If you don't mind going on the fly like that."

"You know I don't."

"Tish has already looked up flight options for you, so just swing by her office on your way out. Thank you."

"You got it."

As I walked down the hallway, my footsteps slowed when I passed Quinn's office. The lights were off, and she had already left. I felt the sting of regret in my chest. I knew Rhys was right. We were avoiding each other. I needed to talk to her. But more than that, I needed to convince her I was worth the chance.

# Chapter Thirty-Seven

# QUINN

*Three days later*

I waved the key card in front of the keypad to my hotel room. Nothing happened. I waved it three more times before I heard the lock click open. I quickly stepped into the hotel room, letting my bag slide off my shoulder in the entryway and tossing the key card on the dresser as I walked past it.

I stopped by the windows and pushed the curtains open to look out over the Seattle skyline glittering in the darkness. I'd taken an unexpected trip here when my father told me he needed help on a commercial fishing case. I tried to explain to him we could've done all of it over video conference, but he preferred the personal touch. He had had a minor medical procedure scheduled for his knee this week and couldn't fly.

The meeting had gone well, and I had one more night here before I flew home. With Christmas a few weeks away now, I felt melancholy.

With a mental shake, I turned away from the

windows. I decided to order room service. I didn't want to go out and see people feeling festive while I felt more alone than I'd ever felt lately.

My friendship with Kenan had become such an integral part of my life over the past five years or so that its absence loomed. Normally, before we'd gone and blown everything up, he might've come with me to Seattle. We would've gotten adjoining rooms and watched a show together. Instead, we weren't even texting and joking. I found out from Tish that he'd left to help Blake in Juneau. Before, he would've texted me he was leaving and sent me photos of funny things. Now, there was a void of silence.

I kept replaying our last conversation at my place and the look of hurt in his eyes. I forced my mind off him. While I waited for my dinner, I logged in to the system where I could select a potential anonymous donor. Every time I tried to do that, my heart ached.

Ever since Kenan had said he wanted me to give him a chance, that was all I could think about.

# Chapter Thirty-Eight

# KENAN

"What do you mean Quinn's gone?" I asked.

Tish blinked up at me. "All she said was she had to go to Seattle for a couple of days."

"For Fireweed Industries?" I prompted.

She shook her head. "No, for personal reasons." The confusion on my face must've been evident. "I would think you would know. You two are usually all up in each other's business," she added dryly.

I didn't know what crossed my face then, but her gaze immediately sobered. "Wise up, Kenan."

"What do you mean?"

"You have been in love with her since you two have been close. I thought maybe you had finally figured it out. But now you're being stupid."

My mouth dropped open before I snapped it shut, muttering, "Oh my God."

Tish cocked her head to the side, the look in her eyes almost pitying. "Kenan, tell Quinn how you feel and make it right. If you're wondering, that's more for your own good. Now, if you don't mind, I have work to do."

Without another word, she tapped her keyboard and returned her attention to her computer screen. I walked down the hallway toward my office, walking by Quinn's office on the way. She must be going to Seattle to do the IVF thing; that had to be it. I had to go find her.

I came to an abrupt stop in the hallway just as Rhys stepped out of his office. "Everything okay?" He stopped in front of me.

"I need to go to Seattle."

"To find Quinn?"

I didn't even care to contemplate how he knew she'd left. "Do you know why she went to Seattle?"

"I actually don't. She told me she needed to go for personal reasons and took a few days off. That's all I know. You should know," he said pointedly.

"Oh, for fuck's sake," I grumbled.

Rhys studied me. "Ask Tish to set up a flight for you and get there tonight. I don't know where Quinn's staying, but I'm sure Tish can find out."

I didn't know how, but I would prove to Quinn that we were worth it before she went and got pregnant from some stranger.

Blessedly, Tish was lightning fast. She made reservations for me and even tracked down where Quinn was staying. "You know she has a favorite hotel there. She refused to let me use the company credit card for her reservations, but I set it up for her."

As I flew down to Seattle on a late evening flight, I prayed I could figure out what to do to prove to Quinn that I loved her and that I wanted a family with her. Every time I did Chase's thought exercise, I nearly broke down at the idea of not having the chance with Quinn. It was far more heartbreaking and terrifying than the prospect of just going for it.

Four hours later, I landed and was grateful that Seattle time was an hour behind Alaska time. As it was, it was coming up on midnight.

I slung my backpack over my shoulder and jogged out of the airport. I hadn't even bothered with getting a car rental, thinking it would be faster to use a car service. In short order, I was pulling up in front of a familiar hotel, the one any of us traveling for Fireweed Industries usually stayed in. I'd had the driver stop by a grocery store so I could get some flowers for Quinn. He had helpfully pointed out there weren't any floral shops open at this hour. I knew Quinn liked flowers. Maybe it wasn't enough, but it was a start.

My heart banged so hard against my ribs that I worried I might actually crack one. I dropped off my bag in the room across the hallway from Quinn's before standing in front of her doorway, flowers in hand and contemplating my entire future.

I knocked, praying she was awake. Before knocking again, I pulled my phone out of my pocket and sent her a text.

**Me:** *I need to see you. I'm here.*

I knocked one more time. Emotions rushed so hard through me that it almost felt as if my body couldn't contain them. I let out an audible sigh when I heard the door opening. A second later, Quinn stood there with her hair in a messy bun, her glasses on, and wearing a big T-shirt that hung halfway down her thighs and a pair of fuzzy socks.

"Quinn." That was all I could say, my voice raspy and my throat tight with emotion.

*Chapter Thirty-Nine*

# QUINN

Kenan stood in the doorway of my hotel room, and all I could do was stare at him. He held a bouquet in his hand. His eyes were wide, and I could've sworn there was a sheen of tears in them.

I didn't realize tears slid down my cheeks until he stepped closer. He lifted a hand, his thumb brushing across my cheek, as he whispered, "Please don't cry. Can I come in?" His hand fell away.

"Of course," I said just as a family walked by.

The woman's eyes widened when she saw me there in my T-shirt and socks. I leaped back, and Kenan stepped inside, closing the door behind him.

We stood there, studying each other. I cataloged his features—the strong line of his jaw, the stubble on his cheeks, his mussed hair, and his bright-blue eyes. My heart felt pierced, the pain of it bittersweet.

"Here." He thrust the bouquet at me. "I know it's not much, and they're not in the best shape because I got them at the grocery store. The guy who picked me up at the airport suggested that because no florists were open at this hour. I love you, and I just needed to do something." Kenan's words came out in a run-on sentence, which was so unlike him.

All the while, my heart pounded so hard I could hear the rush of blood in my ears. I was tingling all over. I took the flowers, smiling so hard my face hurt from it.

"They're beautiful," I said. And they were. It was a bouquet of mostly daisies with some purple flowers scattered among them.

"Also, we're taking the ferry back together," Kenan added.

"We are?" My eyes flew from the flowers back to his face.

He nodded quickly. "Yes. Because we need some time. It's winter, and I'm sure there'll be holiday lights. We can see some wildlife, and that'll give me more than a plane ride to convince you that I really want this with you. I can't imagine life without you. I want a family with you. I love you."

I was still smiling when I hiccupped, and tears splashed on my cheek. Kenan moved closer and wrapped me in his strong embrace. I buried my face in his chest as I cried.

"I don't know why I'm crying," I mumbled against him a few minutes later.

When I leaned back to peer up at him, his cheeks were damp with tears as well.

"I don't know either. I miss you," he said, his gaze boring into mine with such intensity, it took my breath away.

It was my turn to babble. "I missed you. I miss your texts and everything. You haven't sent me a silly picture or a stupid meme or told me what you were annoyed with in too long. I thought we had ruined everything."

I felt him take a deep breath and took my own. Just then, his stomach growled, and I grinned up at him. "Are you starving? Because I was going to order room service, and I never did because I haven't had an appetite, but now I could really use something to eat."

"Let's do it."

Since it was so late, our room service arrived quickly. It felt like old times. We had the television on while lounging on the bed. *That* was a distinction. Before this whole thing started, when we were just friends, we would've been watching a show and laughing about it and eating room service, except we would've been sitting on the couch. Instead, we were on the bed together, stealing little touches here and there. Underlying all of this was a combination of intense emotion spun within the comfort and sturdy foundation of our friendship.

I would probably always wonder if this possibility for us had been there all along, yet we'd both ignored it. Perhaps we hadn't allowed it to flourish because it was too risky, too much of a threat to our friendship that mattered so much.

"Were you asleep?" Kenan asked after we had wheeled the room service cart out into the hallway.

"When?"

"When I knocked on the door."

All we had left from our late-night dinner was a bowl of chocolate mousse, which we had decided to share. Kenan glanced down to carefully scoop some of the mousse.

He held it up for me. "Want a bite?"

"Please." He held the spoon up for me, and I leaned closer. The rich, ridiculously decadent chocolate flavor broke across my tongue, and I couldn't help but moan.

His eyes darkened as he slipped the spoon out of my mouth before helping himself to a bite.

A moment later, he prompted, "You haven't told me if you were asleep."

I met his gaze as I shook my head. "I haven't been sleeping well."

"Neither have I."

"I missed you," I said quietly. The words felt too inadequate to describe just how deeply I'd missed him. My heart tumbled in my chest. I had missed him so *very* much.

Kenan looked at me, quiet for several beats of my heart. He glanced down as he shifted to place the small bowl on the nightstand before turning back to face me.

"I missed you more than I thought it was possible to miss anyone." He lifted a hand, brushing my hair away from my cheek. His fingers slid through the ends of my hair before tracing a line along my collarbone.

Just a single fingertip and his touch felt like fire burning across my skin. I couldn't look away. The moment felt suspended and caught a shimmer of sparks. Another moment later, he shifted closer, whispering against my lips, "I love you, Quinn."

My words were lost in our kiss as he brought his mouth to mine in a slow, sensual kiss. It was the most intense kiss I had ever experienced, a slow, breath-stealing, heart-pounding, claiming kiss. All things considered, it was a good thing we were already on the bed. Because I couldn't have held myself up.

# Chapter Forty

# QUINN

Kenan made love to me. It felt as if every touch shared was a form of communication of sheer, fierce, raw, unguarded love and utterly pure lust.

His palm slid down to cup my breast, and his thumb teased over a nipple. His mouth closed with warm suction over the other nipple. Sparks leaped over my skin as his touch slid over my belly, strong and sure. His fingers dipped between my thighs where I was slick with arousal and near desperate for him.

The brushing sensation of his calloused palm when he pushed my knees apart and dropped kisses like hot honey on the insides of my thighs before he brought his mouth to my sex. He licked into my very core, bringing me to an intense climax until I was trembling all over and pleading for him. Because I needed more. I needed to be joined with him as closely as possible.

Finally, *finally*, he shifted and turned until I was straddling him. He was propped against the pillows, looking deep into my eyes. "Just like this," he whispered.

I felt the thick press of his crown at my entrance as I slid down, slowly sheathing him in the heart of me. I felt the press of his fingertips on my hips as he nudged deeper. "Here, just you, just us," he rasped.

# Chapter Forty-One

# KENAN

I knew Quinn by now, knew the call of her body, knew precisely when her release was building. She bit her bottom lip, her body tightening. She made this little sound in the back of her throat with her breath catching on the hint of a whimper.

"Come for me, sweetheart."

I barely clung to the thinnest thread of control, trying to hold my release at bay until she found hers again. I reached between us with one hand, teasing my fingers over her swollen, slippery wet clit. She cried out sharply, my name following in a ragged pant as her pussy clenched around me.

I finally let go, my release thundering through me like a dam breaking loose, stealing my breath as the pleasure crashed and broke.

Quinn curled against me, and I held her close. We rested like that on the bed, her warm and soft in my lap and my arms holding her in a loose but secure embrace. I could've stayed right here, forever with her.

Eventually, she lifted her head, her eyes meeting mine. "I love you, Kenan Cannon."

# Chapter Forty-Two

# KENAN

Quinn leaned her elbows on the railing of the ferry. The crisp, cold air blew her hair in a swirl. She glanced toward me where I stood at her side, her cheeks pink from the cold as she smiled. "I've never done this trip in the winter."

I leaned over, pressing a kiss to her cheek. "Neither have I."

We'd left Bellingham, Washington, this morning. A seagull called nearby, and we could see a pod of orcas in the distance as they frolicked in the icy ocean waters. This stretch of the journey was dotted with islands, and the coastline was stunning with snow-capped mountain peaks rising tall against the sky and the evergreen trees standing out against the snow flanking them.

Quinn straightened, stuffing her hands in her pockets as she shivered slightly. "Let's go inside," I said, my voice whisked away by the wind.

I slid an arm around her shoulders as we walked back inside. The ferry was decorated for the holidays with lights strung inside the dining area and small wreaths with festive bows mounted at intervals between the booths. I got us some hot chocolate, and we found an empty booth.

Quinn shrugged out of her jacket as she wrapped her hands around the mug, letting out a satisfied sigh. "This is perfect. I'm so glad we took the ferry back. What made you think of that?" she asked after a few sips.

As I looked over at her, my heart felt split wide open, practically beating out of my chest. That was how Quinn made me feel, so vulnerable and raw.

"Because we first made things official on the ferry going to Willow Brook."

Quinn's cheeks flushed pretty and pink. "Official?"

I hadn't planned this, not even a little. Except for one thing. Before I left Fireweed Harbor, I'd stopped by the one and only jewelry store in town and gotten a small ring, thinking I would have it for when I scrambled up the nerve to ask Quinn to marry me. Amethyst was her favorite stone because she loved purple. I figured if she wanted something else, we could get that later.

It was still in my jacket pocket, right where I tucked it before I went to the airport.

"Let's really make it official," I said. My lungs tightened, and my heart kept beating faster and faster.

"What do you mean?"

I slipped my hand into my jacket pocket and pulled out the small ring box. "I got this because I know I want to marry you. Let's just do it. We're on the ferry. We can do it right now. We don't have to do the ceremony now, but I love you, Quinn. I know without even the littlest bit of doubt that I want to spend the rest of my life with you. Let me be the one for you. Please."

Quinn's eyes were wide, and her mouth fell slightly open. She took a shaky breath, and a tear rolled down her cheek as a smile broke across her face.

"Oh my God, Kenan. You remembered," she breathed.

Her eyes dipped down to the ring sitting in the box. It was a platinum band with a simple amethyst set in the center.

"Of course I remembered. I never forget anything when it comes to you."

I slipped out of the booth and knelt on one knee at her side. It was a little cramped, but she turned to face me.

She blinked rapidly. "Yes, yes, yes!"

We'd drawn the attention of the other ferry passengers nearby, and a cheer went up as I slid the ring on her finger.

The next few days were the best days of my life. I knew there would be more of the best days of my life ahead, but I needed this time with Quinn. I had her all to myself. We kept up with our old game of tracking whatever wildlife we saw.

I told Quinn I'd been afraid she had gone to Seattle for IVF treatment. She'd laughed and told me that every time she tried to look at the profiles, all she could think about was me. We decided together we would see what happened the old-fashioned way.

"Are you in a hurry?" I asked on our last night on the ferry.

It was our third night of sleeping in a single bunk together. We kept ourselves busy not sleeping because sleeping comfortably with two people in those narrow bunks was hard.

She wrinkled her nose as she looked up at me. "Well, I am almost thirty. So no, but yes."

I leaned my head against the wall inside the bunk. "What does 'no but yes' mean?"

"Well, now that we're together officially, I know I have time to try to get pregnant. I'm not by myself in this. But there could be issues. I've never tried to get pregnant, so we won't know how it goes until we try."

"We're trying now then, and we'll see what happens."

A part of me was shocked at how easily I had accepted this. Maybe it just had to be Quinn. With her, it was easy. I couldn't imagine a stronger foundation for a lifetime. Oh, I wasn't stupid. In my own life, I'd already experienced enough hurdles and painful experiences that I knew love wasn't all we would need to get through this. I had faith that we could do it together.

Quinn's eyes coasted over my face, a smile teasing the corners of her mouth. "Okay, no but yes, and we'll get started on that right away."

She was laughing when I kissed her.

"Thank you," I said while the ferry docked in Fireweed Harbor.

She leaned back to look up at me. "For what?"

"Letting me be the one."

# EPILOGUE

## McKenna Cannon

I hurried onto the ferry, coming to an abrupt stop as I glanced around. "There won't be enough room," I muttered to myself.

I walked briskly across the deck into the hallway leading to the ferry dining area. Because there was no way to have a private ferry ride, and Kenan and Quinn were bound and determined to have their wedding on the regular ferry route, the planning challenges had been epic.

I was trying to accept that I couldn't control everything for this wedding. It wasn't even my wedding. I walked around the space, eyeing everything beyond my control. They had allowed me to decorate, sparsely, in my opinion.

We were limited with how many guests, and all of them had to be ferry passengers. Fortunately, anyone who was a friend of Kenan and Quinn's would enjoy a ferry ride.

With some arm-twisting, I got permission to use the kitchen for the event. With two world-class chefs as guests, I couldn't stomach, no pun intended, having a cafeteria-style reception. We had a table set up in the center of the dining area. Fiona and David had planned the menu to be easy to prepare and ready as soon as the ceremony was over.

With one last glance around and a check on the status of the food, I raced out of there. Kenan had stayed with Adam last night. Although Quinn insisted she wasn't superstitious, she also said she couldn't spend the night with him the night before the wedding.

As luck would have it, the ferry had needed a maintenance check in Fireweed Harbor. That gave me time to make it all work. I had done some pleading and donated money from Fireweed Industries to the ferry system to make this happen.

The weather was gorgeous. It was summer and warm and pretty. Considering how fickle weather could be, no matter where you were, that stroke of luck relieved me. I hurried down the hallway to check on Quinn. Adam had already texted me to assure me that he would get Kenan here on time. Adam was nothing if not punctual for everything, so I knew he would be on time.

I knocked lightly on the door to the cabin where Quinn was getting ready. Her mother opened the door with a smile. "We're almost ready."

I slipped into the tiny entrance area of the cabin. Quinn looked beautiful.

Pressing my palm to my chest, I blinked back tears. "Quinn! You look amazing. That dress is perfect."

Quinn, definitely more practical than me and not as prone to displays of emotion, turned to face me. "McKenna, you were with me when I tried this dress on. You've already seen it," she pointed out, her smile warm.

"I know, but it's your wedding day."

Quinn took a quick breath, belying her attempt at appearing calm. I stepped forward and reached for both of her hands. "I'm so happy for you and Kenan."

She blinked quickly. "I know you are." Her gaze coasted over me. "You look beautiful too."

"Well, I am your maid of honor. I have to look good."

Quinn giggled, and I squeezed her hands before releasing them. Her mother glanced between us with a smile. "Twenty minutes until go time, right?"

I glanced at my watch. "I need to check on a few more things. Everything else is on schedule. I'm out of here."

I stepped out of Quinn's cabin into the narrow hallway and began walking quickly. I was looking down at my phone, checking to make sure the rest of my family had replied to my group text to confirm everyone was already here or on the way.

A door ahead of me opened, and I literally walked right into it. Hard.

"Ouch!" I stepped back, dropping my phone as I brought a hand to the eye that had bumped into the corner of the door. "I'm sorry!" I exclaimed.

A man appeared from behind the door. My entire system felt zapped with nothing more than a glance at him.

The man in question had almost black hair and startlingly blue eyes. They widened when they landed on me. "You're not the one who needs to apologize. I'm sorry," he said. I held my hand over the eye that was watering from its collision with the edge of the door. "I opened the door right into you. Are you okay?"

He stepped around the door, closing it behind him

and leaning down to pick up my phone. My fingers tingled when he handed it to me. "Let me see." His low tone had a subtle rasp to it.

My insides felt ticklish as hot sparks scattered through me. He lifted a hand, carefully moving mine off my eye. "Oh," he said gently. "You bumped right into that door. I hate to tell you, but I think you'll have some bruising."

I couldn't even speak as I stared at him. I took in his dark brows and the clean, sharp angles of his cheekbones. And, sweet hell, this man had a sexy jaw. I'd never thought any man's jaw was sexy. His was strong, and his chin a little square. He had a hint of stubble, tempting me to run my fingers along the edges of it. His lips were well formed. Lips were nothing I'd *ever* noticed on any human in my life. The upper one had a dip in the middle, and the bottom one was full.

"Are you okay?" he repeated.

My brain finally kicked into gear, like a car that hadn't started suddenly roaring to life. I was mortified because I'd been awestruck by this man.

When he had lifted his hand to check my eye, he had gently moved mine to the side and lowered it. We stood there, sort of holding hands. His grip was warm and dry, and I thought maybe we should keep holding hands forever.

"I'm going to have some bruising?" I belatedly prompted, only then absorbing what he said.

He nodded slowly. "I'm afraid so."

"I'm supposed to be in a wedding."

"You're getting married?" His eyes widened, alarm crossing his face.

"Well, not me," I said quickly. "I'm the maid of honor in my brother's wedding."

"Now?"

"In"—I glanced at my watch—"seventeen minutes."

He studied me for a moment, a tiny grin kicking up one corner of his mouth and sending my belly into a few flips. "Well then, it's a good thing it's soon. Bruising always gets worse later. It'll probably still just be red in about seventeen minutes."

Maybe it was because I had just run into the door, or perhaps it was because I was flustered and in a rush, but it felt like the earth moved, for real. I couldn't bring myself to care all that much. I was stunned.

"Ma'am?" the man standing in front of me prompted.

That kicked through the haze in my brain. "Oh my God. Don't call me ma'am."

He cleared his throat. "I don't know your name."

"It's McKenna. McKenna Cannon." We were still holding hands, and I didn't want to let go.

"Nice to meet you, McKenna. I'm Jack Hamilton."

"Nice to meet you, Jack. Are you going somewhere on the ferry?" I asked.

Once again, a smile teased the corners of his lips. My belly fluttered. I was hot, *really* hot. It had to be my dress.

"Yes. I'm taking the ferry to Diamond Creek. I assume you are as well?"

"Yes, oh yes!" I said quickly.

A door opened just ahead, and my brother Rhys stepped out. He glanced in both directions in the hallway, his eyes landing on Jack and me. I loved knowing his name. Jack was the perfect name for this man.

"McKenna?" Rhys said as he closed the door behind him and began approaching us.

I was so discombobulated it wasn't until Rhys

stopped beside us and dropped his puzzled gaze to where my hand was clinging to Jack's that I realized I was still holding Jack's hand.

I reluctantly released it, smoothing both of my hands down my dress. "What happened to your eye?" Rhys asked.

He looked at Jack, and I quickly interjected. "I was walking down the hallway, looking at my phone when I ran into the door when he came out."

"I think she'll have some bruising," Jack said with an apologetic wince when he glanced toward Rhys.

Rhys studied me, his brows hitching up slightly. "Good thing that ceremony is happening soon."

"That's what I was thinking," I managed.

"Shall we walk down there together?" Rhys prompted.

"Where is Haven?" I asked.

"Already up on deck."

Rhys glanced toward Jack. "Rhys Cannon," he said with a nod.

"Jack Hamilton." Jack dipped his head. When his eyes flicked to me, I felt caught in his gaze.

"If you want to enjoy a wedding," I interjected. "Our brother is getting married up on the deck once we leave the dock."

"It's for everybody?"

"They wanted to get married on a ferry, so that's the deal," Rhys said with a wry grin.

"I might be up there. I usually like to be on the deck when the ferry leaves the dock. The weather is beautiful today," Jack replied.

Rhys and Jack chatted about a few things before Jack glanced my way once more. "Apologies again about the door."

"It truly wasn't your fault. I wasn't paying attention."

With that, Rhys and I said our goodbyes and began walking down the hall.

Just before we stopped at the doorway onto the deck, Rhys asked, "So how is it you ended up holding Jack's hand?"

I stopped and looked up. "How bad does my eye look?"

My brother studied me. "It's red, and a little bruising is showing."

A short while later, Kenan and Quinn pledged their commitment to each other. I temporarily forgot about running into the door and how handsome Jack was. I teared up at the end of the ceremony. I was truly so happy for Kenan and Quinn.

Afterward, I stood on the deck, the wind blowing my hair a little wild. I looked over at Quinn. "You're officially my sister-in-law. I need all the sisters I can get," I teased as I slid my hand through her elbow and squeezed.

Quinn smiled at me. "I'm thrilled to be your sister-in-law."

I let out a happy sigh as I looked around. We had lots of food, enough for all of the passengers. Just then, my gaze landed on Jack. He stood at the corner of the table, talking with my brothers Wyatt, Griffin, and Adam.

"*Great*," I thought to myself.

I didn't realize I'd spoken aloud until Quinn asked, "Great, what? By the way, what's with your eye?"

I grimaced. "I ran into the door when someone was coming out of their room. That guy right over there." I gestured toward Jack.

Quinn glanced over. "Oh. Well, if you're going to run into someone opening the door, it might as well be him. He's pretty easy on the eyes," she said just as Kenan stopped at her side, glancing over in that direction.

"Who is that guy?" he asked. "Rhys said he had something to do with your black eye."

"Oh my God," I ground out. "He was coming out of his room. I was looking at my phone, making sure everybody was coming on time, and I ran into the door with my face."

Kenan burst out laughing. I couldn't help but laugh myself. "It's getting pretty purple." He gestured toward my eye.

"It's fine. It doesn't even hurt anymore." I lifted my hand, gently tapping my fingertips over the surface. It was a little sore, but it really wasn't bad. "I'll be back. I'm going to take a look at it and change."

I hurried down the hallway into my room to change out of my dress into something more comfortable. A few minutes later, I studied myself in the mirror. My eye wasn't that bad, but the skin around it was turning purple. Oh well, oh hell. The wedding was a success, and I had a story.

I exited my room, only to almost collide with Jack walking down the hallway.

He glanced down at me, his gaze holding mine instantly. "Beautiful wedding. Your eye doesn't look too bad."

I shrugged, feeling the heat rise in my cheeks. "I have a black eye, and it's nobody's fault but my own."

"I do feel partially responsible. If I hadn't opened that door right then, you wouldn't have run into it."

I shrugged. "It's okay. Well, I'm sure I'll see you on the ferry again. It's a three-day trip."

"I think I've met your whole family now. You have a big family."

I laughed softly. "There are seven of us, and that's not counting my mom."

"You're all from Fireweed Harbor, I gather?" he prompted.

"We sure are. What brought you to town for a visit?"

"I'm moving there. I'll probably see you once I move."

I had no idea what I said after that. At some point, Jack kept walking down the hallway. He was the first man who'd ever muddled my thoughts like that.

Thank you for reading Kenan & Quinn's story! Want a glimpse of the future for them? Join my newsletter to receive an exclusive scene.

Sign up here: https://BookHip.com/TBCDWDF

p.s. If you are already subscribed, you'll still be able to access the scene.

My next release is Meant to Be, a holiday romance that gets H-O-T when Piper ends up snowed in with her brother's best friend. Small problem: there's only one bed.

One-click to pre-order Meant To Be - due out Nov 16, 2023!

Up next in the Fireweed Harbor Series is One More Time.

McKenna ends up with a black eye when she meets Jack. Sort of, but not really, his fault.

Black eye aside, the earth shakes when she meets him.
But McKenna only believes in love for other people.
Unlucky might as well be her middle name.

Jack doesn't care about luck and he's a breath-stealing,
swoony hotshot firefighter. He can't forget McKenna,
although she makes him forget plenty of other things.

Don't miss McKenna & Jack's swoony, hot and intense
romance!

One More Time - due out February 2024!

For more swoony romance...

This Crazy Love kicks off the Swoon Series - small
town southern romance with enough heat to melt you!
Jackson & Shay's story is epic - swoon-worthy &
intensely emotional. Jackson just happens to be Shay's
brother's best friend. He's also *seriously* easy on the
eyes. Shay has a past, the kind of past she would most
definitely like to forget. Past or not, Jackson is about
to rock her world. Don't miss their story! Free on all
retailers!

Burn For Me is a second chance romance for the ages.
Sexy firefighters? Check. Rugged men? Check.
Wrapped up together? Check. Brave the fire in this
hot, small-town romance. Amelia & Cade were high
school sweethearts & then it all fell apart. When they
cross paths again, it's epic - don't miss Cade's story!
Free on all retailers!

For more small town romance, take a visit to Last
Frontier Lodge in Diamond Creek. A sexy, alpha SEAL

meets his match with a brainy heroine in Take Me Home. Marley is all brains & Gage is all brawn. Sparks fly when their worlds collide. Don't miss Gage & Marley's story!
Free on all retailers!

If sports romance lights your spark, check out The Play. Liam is a British footballer who falls for Olivia, his doctor. A twist of forbidden heats up this swoon-worthy & laugh-out-loud romance. Don't miss Liam & Olivia's story.
Free on all retailers!

# FIND MY BOOKS

**Thank you for reading Be The One! I hope you enjoyed the story. If so, you can help other readers find my books in a variety of ways.**

1) Write a review!

2) Sign up for my newsletter, so you can receive information about upcoming new releases & receive a FREE copy of one of my books: http://jhcroixauthor.com/subscribe/

3) Like and follow my Amazon Author page at https://amazon.com/author/jhcroix

4) Follow me on Bookbub at https://www.bookbub.com/authors/j-h-croix

5) Follow me on Instagram at https://www.instagram.com/jhcroix/

6) Like my Facebook page at https://www.facebook.com/jhcroix

**Fireweed Harbor Series**
Make You Mine
Dare To Fall
Be The One
One More Time - due out February 2024!
**Light My Fire Series**
Wild With You
Hold Me Now
Only Ever Us
Fall For Me
Keep Me Close
With Every Breath
All It Takes
Take Me Now
**Dare With Me Series**
Crash Into You
Evers & Afters
Come To Me
Back To Us
Take Me There
After We Fall
**Swoon Series**
This Crazy Love
Wait For Me
Break My Fall
Truly Madly Mine
Still Go Crazy
If We Dare
Steal My Heart
**Into The Fire Series**
Burn For Me
Slow Burn
Burn So Bad
Hot Mess
Burn So Good

Sweet Fire
Play With Fire
Melt With You
Burn For You
Crash & Burn
That Snowy Night
**Brit Boys Sports Romance**
The Play
Big Win
Out Of Bounds
Play Me
Naughty Wish
**Diamond Creek Alaska Novels**
When Love Comes
Follow Love
Love Unbroken
Love Untamed
Tumble Into Love
Christmas Nights
**Last Frontier Lodge Novels**
Take Me Home
Love at Last
Just This Once
Falling Fast
Stay With Me
When We Fall
Hold Me Close
Crazy For You
Just Us

# ACKNOWLEDGMENTS

I often think my acknowledgments are redundant because I keep thanking many of the same people. Well, that's how it is! It still matters.

My readers are why I write stories. Thank you for staying with me on this journey, loving my characters and asking for more. Really.

I am blessed with a fabulous team. My editor who sometimes makes me giggle with clarifying questions. My proofreader who has lots of patience with my tendency to change side character names mid-book. Who does that? Me! My cover designer, Najla Qamber, for patience, kindness and a much better eye than me. The bookstagrammers, bloggers, booktokers and more who keep shouting out their love for romance far and wide. I and many authors and readers are so very grateful.

To DBC, my dogs, and my family. Love you lots!

xoxo

J.H. Croix

# ABOUT THE AUTHOR

USA Today Bestselling Author J. H. Croix lives in a small town somewhere with her husband and two spoiled dogs. Croix writes contemporary romance with sassy women and alpha men who aren't afraid to show some emotion. Her love for quirky small-towns and the characters that inhabit them shines through in her writing. Take a walk on the wild side of romance with her bestselling novels!

*Places you can find me:*
jhcroixauthor.com
jhcroix@jhcroix.com

facebook.com/jhcroix
instagram.com/jhcroix
bookbub.com/authors/j-h-croix